stories by Bonnie Chau

2040 BOOKS

an imprint of

Library of Congress Cataloging-in-Publication Data
Names: Chau, Bonnie, author.
Title: All roads lead to blood : stories / Bonnie Chau.
Description: Santa Fe, NM : SFWP, 2018.
Identifiers: LCCN 2017060750 (print) | LCCN 2018014487 (ebook) | ISBN 9781939650887 (e-pdf) | ISBN 9781939650894 (epub) | ISBN 9781939650900 (mobi) | ISBN 9781939650870 | ISBN 9781939650870 q(pbk. : alk. paper)
Subjects: LCSH: Chinese Americans—Fiction. | LCGFT: Short stories.
Classification: LCC PS3603.H3825 (ebook) | LCC PS3603.H3825 A77 2018 (print) | DDC 813/.6--dc23
LC record available at https://lccn.loc.gov/2017060750

Published by 2040 Books, an imprint of the Santa Fe Writers Project
369 Montezuma Ave #350
Santa Fe, NM 87501
www.sfwp.com

Find the author at www.bonniechau.com

Contents

To my family.
And to all my past and current loves, secret and not.

What would the audience say if I gave birth to such creatures?

—Yoko Tawada, *The Naked Eye,*
translated by Susan Bernofsky

Monstrosity

ARTHUR APOLLO ASHER and I met at the boba shop called Boba-Go-Banana. We sat outside drinking and chewing through our boba milk teas—mine was the Go Banana one, it was yellow-gray, and had a sick sweetness to it. The afternoon was sunny, with a smooth, cold breeze. The shop was in the Heritage Crest strip mall, which was on the corner of the intersection of Culver Drive and Irvine Center Drive. The outside of it was peach-colored stucco, and it was this peach-colored stucco because the whole strip mall was this way.

We watched zigzagging Chinese drivers creating a hell out of the parking lot. It was The Garden of Earthly Delights, if all the fang-limbed monstrosities were cars, and if all the acid lime green grass and baby blue-eyed waters were the asphalt. I said something about this, and Arthur Apollo Asher smiled and lifted his shoulders.

"They're your people," he said.

"It's alienating," I said. But I didn't know if they were the aliens or if I was the alien. We talked a little bit about San Francisco, where we had met while we were both still in school, through mutual friends of his brother's, or was it through family friends. He said he was sorry to hear about my grandfather. I nodded. I didn't say anything about it. I looked at him, at the matte opacity of the pale skin under his eyes, at the way his hands cradled the plastic cup, at the way his lips tightened around the fat straw. We had done it, several times, years ago, once while drunk and stoned, a couple times just stone cold sober.

Afterwards, I got into Arthur Apollo Asher's lowered, kitted-out, spoiler-winged Acura NSX. Of course it was white, of course it was referred to as White Rice, and of course his possession of it was only legitimized by the fact that he had inherited it, an heirloom of the late nineties, from his adopted Chinese wannabe-gangster brother. He was so embarrassed about it, but also proud, the way you might be proud of inheriting a bro-y pickup truck from Huntington Beach because you are so obviously not that kind of person, that it's *funny*, or something, or so you imagine. He grinned his bared teeth confidently at me as I got in—bucket seat, race car seat belts, the harness a silent spider on my body. I found myself aroused by the pieces of gleaming metal, flat like puzzle pieces, sleek and Richie Rich.

He zoomed over to his house on Barranca Drive, shifting gears as if he was in a movie, and slipped the White Rice rocket, fist into glove, into an ultra specific spot on the driveway. I followed him up the stairs into the bedroom, and the first thing he did, was walk toward me but then away from me, and I looked over and he was walking to the wall behind me to flick down the light switch. It was dark now, but not that dark, because the lights were still on in the rest of the house, lighting the marble floors and granite countertops, the thick carpeting on the stairs. Being in a house like this, everything brand new, made me feel like I was in high school again. I had not been back to Irvine in a very long time, in six years maybe. I had not felt this me—this obedient, unquestioning me which was only alive when placed in a peach-colored stucco building—had not felt her simultaneous foreignness and familiarity, her desperation—in a very long time. I was an amorphous putty again, in the hands of my parents, shaped as a dutiful daughter. I was one Chinese girl in a pile of them again, average height average weight straight black hair brown eyes. People don't know this secret, and this secret is that peach-colored stucco has the power to suck out all of what makes you you, all of your individual identity, all your creativity and aesthetics. It's better that way, it's easier to swallow. Less stuff sticking out and into the sticky gummy back of your throat.

Arthur Apollo Asher put his hands around my hips, and pressed his fingertips against my butt cheeks. I was wearing a red skirt, of respectable length, that did nothing for me, but I thought, well, respectability is something. Maybe. Maybe it is something, something I have only heard of. I made this joke in my head, kind of smiled. He pressed harder, and I imagined his fingers slightly sinking into soft pale flesh, shadows blooming like a flower around his fingertips, growing out of nothing, out of skin pressing skin, an instantaneous moat of dark, the appearance of depth. Pants and skirts were shrugged, scooted down, buttonholes were stretched into O's like gasping mouths, then relieved of their charges. I stepped up onto his bed, and stood, poised royally for a fight. He pushed me up against the wall, placed his penis against the opening of my vagina. He held the base, guiding it like a flashlight, where to go, what to do? What to see?

I wanted him, I did not want him, his penis, inside of me, I was not sure. Who was this guy? His name was Arthur Asher Astrophel, or what was it again. He would be the closest thing to a Chinese guy I had sex with, and that wasn't saying much—he only drove a rice rocket and had an adopted Chinese gangster brother—but it was saying something that might finally make sense, make my perceptions more whole, more solid. But here, here, I pulled him forward violently, almost a stumble of feet and toenails, and somehow he fell up into me, cockfirst, as if driving a sword upward with full intent to disembowel.

He regained his balance, bent his knees, and then unbent them as he stood unsteadily like a shivering, just-birthed animal. He moved back up, pushed his prick up into me more deeply, pricking as far as he could go, and I was pushed up, pushed up a groan, as if this thrust up inside of me had in turn displaced out of my belly, then chest, then throat, then mouth, a sound, like this. I slumped down, started slumping down, falling, bringing him with me, until we were sitting, entangled on his bed, and then he fell back on his back. He flipped me over slightly so I was on my stomach, moved over me, found a condom somewhere without going anywhere, pushed himself inside of me from behind, I moaned, a long and deep, wanton, want, want, wanting, keeling, keening sound, low and wet, this was sex, this was it, sex—God, society, humanity, flesh—it all made sense, or at least it all was okay, or it was okay that none of it made sense.

I turned back around, and then I felt something I had never felt before, and certainly people feel things for the first time all the time, but this, I mean, I strained up, against Arthur Apollo Asher's shoulder, which was sinewy and had clamped on it, like a starfish to a face, a holy map of holy trails across holy lands. This was his description and not mine, and I didn't question it because some things unravel so quickly under questioning. I had asked him the first time I saw it, where the Silk Road was in this sprawling map of a tattoo, and what about the Trail of Tears, and he had frowned something about not being holy, and I had laughed instead of panicking that he didn't understand what I wanted to talk about.

But now I cried out because I was not sure who this guy was, who had suddenly become a part of something scary, whose mouth hung slightly open above me, eyes shut as if to better concentrate on panting to a finish. We had looked at each other over boba and I had not been able to find even the tiniest chime of understanding or knowledge resonating in his eyes. He did not see me at all, except for the narrow path of light that his penis had illuminated. My heart started beating very quickly, and there was the sound of tearing, sound waves threatening to vibrate the tiny cilia of my ears. It was a very distinct paper or fabric ripping sound, fibers parting, right at the entrance of my hearing. What I felt, though, was not a tearing, but a rapid separating from head to toe, as if of evaporating skin, and a shocking pleasure at the plunge into coldness. I imagined waving my hands around cartoonishly up in the air and exclaiming, "I am not a virgin! There should be no tearing!" but here it was, something wrested, an irrevocable estrangement of me from me. One Pisces fish swimming there, the other there, a string in between, unraveling to a jarring snap of nothing.

My orgasm split wide and then clamped shut, and my eyes opened suddenly, the wave of oxygen hitting my corneas. I could feel my eyeballs darting around, not seeing anything, but switching back and forth in the semi-darkness, with nowhere to look, moving around, as if they could look inwards, and were peering into my brain: what happened, why did that feel like that, if something was being split open, what was going to come out, what was going to encounter the light and air of day for the first time?

And then, we were lying there, on his bed, and I saw that I could see myself in the mirror on the closet by his bed. I looked over again, and realized that there was not a mirror there, but that it was just me, standing there. That there was somehow another me, a non-mirror me, who did not copy me as in a reflection, but who just stood there. I sat up. I put my hands on my flushed thighs, pressed at the protrusions of my kneecaps, covered my tits with my right forearm. She looked at me. She seemed pale. Her face was a little crooked, but I guess that was only because I was seeing a real me, and not a mirror-image me. She stood differently. She had better posture, a real backbone. I looked again, and she looked back at me, unflapped. Of course, why would she care, she was a creature, a mythological beast, and I was just some person.

Finally, she spoke. "You be me, and I'll be the other you," she said. I liked her voice immediately, it was not like mine, not even like hearing a recorded version of mine. Not so low and wavery, not like a clown at all, not a sour sounding voice.

"What do you mean?" I asked. She shook her head, her hair was my hair, but better, more unified, it swung with purpose. She stared at me wearily, I was wearing her out, and it had only been one minute, and she was me. I put my mouth in a sheepish shape.

"We will both be you," she said, saltily, "and it will be so much better for us. You be one you, and I'll be the other, we will contradict each other, but not ourselves."

"Oh," I said, "oh." I tried out a nod. My neck felt unused. Achitophel Asher Apollo what's-his-name snored, but I could not think about him anymore. Who cared about him, when I had somehow been split into two.

"Listen," she said, "This way, there won't be this problem of one part of you trying to get away from the other. We can get away from each other at any time, no problem-o."

"Oh, yes," I said. "Right. Yes. Okay. But," I said.

"Wait, listen," she said, slowly, like a dissolving Saltine. I leaned forward in the bed. "I will be the Chinese you."

"You will?" I said, taken aback. "What does that mean?" She squinted. "What do I be then?" I asked. In my brain, I tested out those five words again, the words strung together like the cold beads of a necklace, *What do I be then*. I was fighting hard to keep track of what was going on. I took an ocean-sounding breath.

The Chinese me looked at me. I saw that she was already the Chinese me, more impassive, wore sunblock all the time. She had implacable ideas. She laughed to hide. She sneered in place of any gesture of tenderness. "Where does that leave me?" I asked. I needed to know. "If you take away my Chinese me, do I become neutral? A planet of foggy translucence like a tapioca ball? Or white? Maybe I become white?"

She scoffed. "No. No no. You know nothing. You know you have problems with the Chinese you. I will just be the Chinese you *for you*. You won't have to think about it at all."

I looked down at my hands, which I did not remember clasping together. Maybe I had been waiting all my life for someone to say that to me. I looked at her. I wanted to test her. She must have known what I was thinking. She nodded her chin up at me. I stood up obediently. Although she was paler, she was more substantive, solid. I watched my left hand reaching over into the space between us, slowly toward the defiant slope of her shoulder, right below the jutting glow of her collarbone, my fingers outstretched, wanting to see what her skin felt like, what it would be like to touch the Chinese me.

But the story ends here, several inches before denatured skin meets I'll-never-know-what skin, because that is when I started to disappear, molecules of air replacing molecules of skin and blood and fat and bone. I was disappearing, in that dim and shadow-filled suburban bedroom, disappearing faster the closer I got to her. But I didn't stop, I didn't stop.

Medusa Jellyfish

AGAINST THE WHITE sky, dozens of pigeons fly, tiny crosses turning into stars, then flattening, veering, tiny stars, tiny crosses, flicking, flickering, crossing and uncrossing, and then a stomach-dropping swoop.

There is a sudden movement by Rhiannon's feet. She sees first, in the odd shape of red, a small puddle of blood, before she realizes it's a roundish leaf that has blown down and pooled. More dry bit-edged leaves, crumbling and crisp, scrape-drag along the gray sidewalks. It is not yet the month to put on gloves, so Rhiannon's hands naturally fold into fists, half withdrawn into her jacket sleeves. Fists, ready. Fists, withdrawing. Everywhere she looks, people and plants have been sucked dry, fast-motion decay, flesh withering, fruit withering, gristle and fat slurped gone. The one last suck through the straw, quick, blinding, stinging of a whip, gone in a blink.

Her body is in a disequilibrium of cold and hot. Warm under her down jacket, cold legs, heated feet stuffed into wool socks (thin, not yet the month for thick), leather boots (thin, not yet the month for snow). Some people are wearing wool hats, some people are wearing knit gloves. Some people are wearing T-shirts, and wish they were not, wish they were hot.

She fixes her eyes straight ahead, she is deeper inside herself now, for fall. Her body is the same size, but she, herself, has shrunken small, curled fetal, a mere pea inside this body. This is the first fall. The first-ever fall of her life. When people talk about seasons, it's not just the season, but the transition from the last one to the current one, that they are actually talking about. Spring is not spring, but the change from winter to spring. And fall, this is something else. She has never had this before, never seen it, never felt it like this. During her travels and years abroad, she had experienced seasons several times before, but only fall-winter-spring-summer. She had never done summer to fall.

It is the worst of them all. The biggest fall, descent into madness, startled at being yanked out of woozy warmth and sweat-dripping heat. It is like being slapped. The sudden burn of submersion into an ice cold pool. But no water. An ice cold vacuum. An ice cold glass. Clear, translucent, nothing but air and wind.

The Jellyfish Appears

It is a Wednesday. She remembers this because Wednesdays are the most watery of days, suspended midweek. Bells somewhere were chiming 9:30 a.m. The M train rolls by, the bedroom window screen is pixelated from the rain outside, a smeary, near-sighted blur.

Rhiannon is holding her phone, not one of the flat heavy ones that can do everything, the ones that feel like you are holding a window pane of glass balanced in your palm, but a small plasticky one, that she squeezes in her right hand, as if it is a person, the one person whose calls and voicemails and text messages she wishes were the actual person, not just something to read or something to hear.

When the rain stops, she opens the door to her bedroom. It is also a door from her bedroom. The kitchen light is on. Not the stove one, which she and her roommates leave on when they are full of time and deliberation and can expend the mental and physical effort to be atmospheric. But the actual overhead light, which is less forgiving. It screams of emptiness. She slips her feet into her yellow flats, they make a flat slapping sound on the hardwood. She turns the brass doorknob of the front door. She walks down the hallway, which is jointed at several intervals, like walking the perimeter of an octagon. She walks in a straight line, watching the grain of the hardwood floors. They are worn, gentle.

She pushes the heavy metal door out into the stairwell, and pulls it clicked behind her. She walks up two more flights of stairs to the very top landing. She pushes that metal door out, and carefully steps over the raised part of the wall. The roof is empty. It is always empty. But above the ledges all around, the city stands, all around, it is everywhere.

She walks to the edge of one side, and lights her cigarette. She walks to another side. She walks along one entire side, looking out over the wall to see if there is anyone she knows walking down below on the sidewalks. There is nobody. There is something far off in the distance, on the far edge of the Manhattan skyline, that looks like the leftover blaze of an orange sunset, or like the afterglow of fireworks. No matter how much she squints or blinks, tries to refocus her eyes, she cannot make out what it is. She sits down on the ledge on the far corner, and looks at the city, mostly at the city on the other side of the river.

She goes back inside, and steps into her half bathroom. She turns on the faucet and a first squiggle of jelly comes out like water. Like one drop of water, that stretches itself, stretches itself into slow motion beyond-time goo. It is perfectly clear, perfectly crystalline and defined. A cartoon. Slowly, a jellyfish pours itself out, like a dainty woman's leg and foot lowering onto the ground from behind an open car door. Rhiannon looks at it, does not wrap her head around any of it, looks and looks, synapses firing away, nothing hitting anything, nothing connecting with anything, nothing known in the known universe is familiar with this. She pulls the faucet handle closer to her, it gloops out faster.

She has eaten jellyfish before. At Chinese banquet dinners, sometimes it comes in a small compartment on a large cloisonné platter, soy-browned translucence in an unceremonious pile. Put a little bit of it on the plate, turn the lazy Susan, move on to the next dish, let it pass to the next person, rotate. It's cool on the tongue, slightly sweet, a soft crunch, like thin cartilage.

She has seen washed-up Portuguese man-of-wars before, faded blue and delicate as bubbles, emerging lifelessly from the sands of beaches on other continents. She has seen ghostly box jellyfish pumping in slow, graceful motion in circular aquarium tanks. She has never seen one come out of a sink faucet.

She walks into the kitchen and pulls out a big glass mason jar and a clinking metal lid and walks back into the bathroom. The jellyfish is still slinking itself out of the faucet spout, taking its sweet jelly time, lowering deliberately, the way she usually lowers herself into water, from air—here, into air, from water. The jellyfish is the color of a bruise. Rhiannon has only ever seen a bruise from the other side of skin, and tries to imagine how it must really be, on the inside of skin, inside the body, a blue planet suspended in flesh and fat, marble-clear. This jellyfish, it is blue like the inside of a bruise. Each layer is a transparency, edges fluttery like lace, the swirled hem of a ruffled skirt dipped in bloody blue ink.

She cannot bring herself to scoop it up and let it fall, trapped, into the glass jar, so instead she reaches her hand into the sink and brushes it to the side, while she plugs the drain and lets the water fill up. She needs to figure out what to wear to work, or she will be late. Last Thursday, she had showed up at work, muttered "morning" to the delivery guys outside fiddling with their bikes, and stepped carefully down the old stone stairs at the back of the restaurant. She pulled locker doors open and slammed them shut, metal slamming, one after another, until she found the emptiest one, even then, with bunched-up dirty checkered pants at the bottom. She threw her purse in, shrugged off her sweater and jacket together in one piece, tossed that in, used her foot to kick the pile in further, and shut the door. When she got back upstairs, she swung the door into the kitchen to see what she could bring back out to the floor.

Rhiannon Tells Hank about Bo Shen

She saw Bo Shen in the kitchen, he was tall. He was standing on the other side of the counter, head bent down, chopping something.

Oh God, Hank says. They are sitting on the M train, going across the bridge.

No, listen, she says. Bo Shen was standing there, and did not look up. There were a few other cooks doing some prep work, or sitting, resting on industrial restaurant supply plastic pails. Bo Shen stood there, and she wanted him to look up. They had never exchanged any words before, what language would their words be in, if they did? Well, presumably, Chinese, since, like everyone else in the kitchen, he didn't speak English. She couldn't even remember if she had ever said 謝謝 to him, which she did usually to the cooks, when she was waiting to run food out, and someone slid a plate onto the expediting counter.

Bo Shen had disappeared suddenly back in June, because he had been fired. He had started seeing the cute big-eyed ponytailed food-packer girl, who was very sweet indeed, and who used to always guilelessly ask Rhiannon to translate newspaper job listings for her, and then it had turned out that he had a girlfriend, and this girlfriend had shown up at the restaurant one day, and started screaming at him, had stormed through the entire front of the restaurant, into the back kitchen, screaming, and then followed him downstairs, screaming, and then the food-packer girl had shown up for work, and the girlfriend really lost it then, and dragged Bo Shen back upstairs and back onto the restaurant floor, and Rhiannon isn't sure what happened then, but she knows he disappeared after that.

She can see this scene very clearly. She can see him, within this scene, very clearly, hooded eyes, an insolence clearly set on his unyielding cheeks. She sees him standing there facing his girlfriend, taking it, her screams and pushes hitting him like hitting a wall, he takes it, is pushed back and back, he is almost, almost smirking, he almost finds this funny, this prissy girlfriend of his, throwing such a hysterical fit.

He is the kind of guy, sallow-skinned, looks like a butcher, like he isn't outside too much, maybe just to play basketball once in a while, a twenty-five-year-old with dark-shadowed bags under his eyes. In the wet swelter of summer, his pant legs are messily rolled up, his white collared short-sleeved button-down dishwasher shirt barely even buttoned, his stare dead-on when she finally manages to catch its flicker. He is unsmiling, smokes cigarettes outside leaning against the door of the next building, his Chinese is slow and assured, low and full of profanities that sound only vaguely familiar to her. He is full of secrets that could fuck you up, but he was in no hurry. She couldn't guess what his life might be like, at all. But he had a girlfriend. And a food-packing mistress. And now he had been fired. And now he had been rehired.

Rhiannon and Hank Were in Love, Once

Hank is shaking his head at her. What do you think of the concept, slumming it? he asks her. She looks at him. What? she says. He is nodding now, nodding at his own thoughts, at what he is about to say to her, even though she knows, she knows he has no right to say anything to her, they were in love once, and back then they had rights to say anything, and now nothing means much anymore.

Remember when you dated that frat boy, Thomas? he is saying, nodding. What do you call that?

Slumming? she says, taking the bait. You think that was slumming?

Yes, he says. You thought he was beneath you, we all thought he was beneath you, and you knew it, and you liked him because of it. He was a fucking beefcake. He was on so many intramural sports teams, which is fine, but it's only fine if you do other shit too. It's only fine if you're not a fucking philistine. It's only fine if you also like art and read books and listen to some music besides fucking Tom Petty.

I like Tom Petty, she says. She sounds like she's whining. Thomas had been amazing, he'd been a bartender, and had more social graces and skills of engagement, than all her other friends put together.

So what about you dating me? she says. She is not sure why she says this. It just comes out.

What do you mean? Hank says.

Well, she says. Don't you think you were slumming it a little bit, she says. She doesn't really know what she is saying.

Um. He waits for her.

On a more subconscious level, she says. Because I'm Asian. I bet on some level you were attracted to some sort of debasing ancestral stereotype, you know, poor Chinese village beauty, working out in the fields, subsumed by filial piety, living with these backwards traditions, who turns out to be really good at sucking cock.

Wow, Hank says.

What, she says. You started it. Why do we need to dissect my attraction to Bo Shen? Why did you have to call that slumming?

You're aligning yourself with rural poverty? And claiming that you're really good at sucking cock? he says.

Stop it, she says.

He raises his eyebrows halfway up. She looks away.

But at Some Point, Hank Moved Away from Rhiannon

I think I'm moving to New York, Hank said, and he said it right there, on that couch, that yellow couch on which they had done everything.

Rhiannon stared at him. She ran the tip of her tongue, pressing the pink wormy muscle, over the sharp hard edges of her upper front teeth, back and forth. Palate. Cleft. Gums. Soft. Hard. Her eyes were dry and still. Like they belonged to an unblinking doll. The couch, she didn't have to look at it, she would remember forever that exact shade of yellow, mustardy, the faintest of designs on it, geometric, some acid green jagged lines and zig zags. She didn't have to look at it, and she didn't, she looked at him, she had not moved.

He was moving. Moving. Moving, moving, putting his body, his self, away, taking it far from her, putting it in a city on the other side of the country. She thought about all the things she should say, that would allow her to preserve a sense of who she was, what person she had chosen to present herself as, to the world, how she was, who she was, mostly though, mostly, what she meant was: what kind of girl she was.

She would say, You should do whatever you need to do. We all do what we have to do. She would shrug. She would be a combination of things—a juxtaposition of things—to show the world that this was what she was, because this was what all people were: things that were the opposites of themselves, things that should not be next to each other, but were.

She would shrug her nonchalance, but stare directly into his eyes her fervor.

She said, You don't owe me anything. You should move to New York. Good for you. It's good to move.

That was the big one. *It's good to move.*

I think that's a really good idea. She said it, and as she said each word, as each word slipped from her lips like a gold coin, she believed it. She believed it, she believed it, it was good to move, move or die.

What she was interested in, was "escape." That little button at the top corner of the computer keyboard. And also, especially, "shift." They were magical words made technological and dull, magical words whose magic you could only see if you remembered to see.

Escape felt necessary, warranted, legitimate, while an escapist seemed blameworthy, seemed to be a character flaw. An escapist was a problem, an escape was a solution.

Broadway-Lafayette

Stand clear of the closing doors please, the voice says. The doors stay open.

How, Hank wants to know, did it happen? How did he lose her? Years later, they both know he was the one who moved away, he made the move to leave her, but she had already done most of the work of removing herself.

Inch by inch, she says. And then, nothing. The end, my friend. She had been nineteen. They had taken turns scarring each other, and all she had wanted was more. What proof did she have of life, aside from this? What did she have, aside from her body, and what showed on her skin?

Rhiannon wants to change the subject. She wants to talk about something that is less interesting, less likely to blow up, requires less attention, because the jellyfish in the sink has started to take up all the space in her head. At first, she had been afraid it might turn out to be a huge creature, but by the time she was ready to leave for work, it had finished glooping out, and floated comfortably in the water-filled sink.

There Was Hank's Wedding Incident

Rhiannon had gone alone to Hank's wedding, at a winery-ranch-estate somewhere between Malibu and Santa Barbara. At the reception, Hank's best man was asking her why, again, she refused to date guys from Middle America. It's like...Middle Earth, she explained drunkenly, despite her complete ignorance of anything about Tolkien or LOTR, which she was referring to as LOADER. It's an alien planet, she continued. Or an alien stratum. Of earth. Or unearthly existence. All these people with no exposure to or interest in diversity. No Chinese food. Or avocados.

She paused. She took another sip of her watery whiskey. She was in bad shape, this was bad form, but she couldn't stop, she could go on for quite some time, this was one of her favorite topics, America. I know I make a big stink about being open-minded about accents, she began again, but I really don't like it when they pronounce bags, begs. At this, Hank's sister gasped out a laugh, a hiccuping type of laugh with her eyes fluttering shut.

Because it was a wedding, and it was Hank's wedding, and because she was drunk and because there happened to be a moment when cornering was easy, she cornered him by the restrooms.

So, am I the last person you had sex with before you got married? she said. The last person you had sex with before you started having sex with the only person you'll have sex with for the rest of your life? is what she meant. He looked at her. She had to say something more, because he said nothing. Do you think about that? she asked.

Well, I think we both know that you made sure I wouldn't really care enough to think about that.

She gave him a look—she didn't even have to make an effort, she didn't even change her expression to be anything, really, it was not even a look, as much as it was just her turning her head to look at him, widely blank and blind, as if looking with the whites of her eyes—before turning back to her table and the poor excuse for a cake.

She knew what he was talking about. Still, she was surprised that he'd said it. If he had been able to say things like that when they were not-together, things might have been quite different.

There Was the Incident in which Rhiannon Had a Fling with Her Twenty-Year-Old Intern

Someone was being flung against something, all right. A bird against a glass building. Who was doing the flinging?

In the middle of the coffee shop was an unusually large group of people standing. They were talking loudly and looked as if they had been product-placed into the scene. Make a scene where young people in their twenties and thirties are really cool, make it a mixture of ragged-looking people with advanced degrees in philosophy and film studies and ragged-looking people who dropped out of high school to follow Animal Collective around the world.

Rhiannon stood to the side of the counter while three baristas and two sandwich-makers ignored her. They were busy. After she ordered, she stood to the other side of the counter. She poured herself a plastic cup of water from the small cooler that had several slices of cucumber floating at the top.

This had started because Chris, her intern, had wanted to be her friend. He had very urgently prescribed a necessary meeting, outside of this, *this*, he gestured to the workspace around them, and oh she had said, oh yes, frowning a little as if she, too, felt this urgency. And she thought she did. She, too, was frustrated, perturbed that all they had, so far, was *this*.

Oh, I'm pretty particular about my meat, he told her conspiratorially, from across the tiny table. Didn't he know better. Couldn't he control his smile, his warm sick happy eyes, whenever she said anything to him, whenever she relented her eyes to meet his eyes. In a comic strip, his smile, as he looked up at her, might have been illuminated with a blank white asterisk of movie-star flash. Shhure, she said, smiling big back at him. All week while she had been unsmiling, she had been saving up for these hours of interminable goodwill.

In her imagined version of the scene, she said, Look, I know, or I think I know what it is you want from me, you want to be that kind of close. You want to share the mundane details and pleasantries and small talk and asking-after that are the tiny things that build up something that, even if it did disappear someday, wouldn't be able to do so without a trace. And, she said, I know this, and maybe before I could be or give or do that, and maybe someday again, but not right now, right now my pockets are empty, don't you see, my eyes are empty too.

In her imagined version, she said something like that. She explained, even if I want you to know me, even when I really want it and am trying, even then, I can't not hold something back. And so what hope do you have here, if I don't even care for you to know me? What hope? None. *I am not trying to give you any hope.*

In the din of the coffee shop, in the din of his worried rambling about job prospects, she leaned forward and said, don't freak out. It's totally going to be fine.

In a Little While

They have on their hands a perfect morning. It starts out warm, then cools, dims. Surprisingly dark, as if the lights have been turned off. It is startling on the skin to feel such coolness, the wind whispering in through the window screen, the glass pushed all the way up.

She shows Hank the jellyfish in her sink, and then they sit next to each other in her room.

The bedroom door is wide open. The overcast light feels pure, clean, flooding the room with a forgiving glow, lean and tender soft shadows. Green things are watered, other things are straight, swept, in their places. All they have to do is lean back on the couch in the corner. Outside, her housemate is making coffee, talking on the phone, clomping around in his boots.

A flash of lightning, it starts to pour. She leans on the sill to look out the window. Outside the entrance of the daycare preschool across the corner, a boy in a red sweatshirt is turning around and around in the rain, with both of his arms stretched out. Thunder, the cool breeze, the sticky sound of tires on a raincoated asphalt.

Basil and mint sit in the window. Faded sheer red curtains push with small graceful movements. The blood clot blister she had on her finger from getting it caught in the door at work has dried up, peeled away. The rain stops. She would like to show him the roof—they could have a cigarette up there. They could eat some salad, hard-boil some eggs and eat them salty, talk about the jellyfish.

They go up on the roof, it is like coming up from out of warm bathwater, into oxygen, into air, into something manageable and free. They gulp it down, soak it in. They comment on how nice it is outside, up there, about how it feels like California. They say this numerous times, not even bothering to rephrase, or change their words in the slightest way or order.

Stevie Versus The Negative Space

IN ORDER TO SEE the shape of Stevie, start here, with the shapes of the guys. Her first boyfriend in college was Mexican. Her first boyfriend called her Jelly Barbarella. She was twenty, he was twenty-six, and she was like so what, to her friends, to the world, a world in which six years was something to gawk about. It was not a creative world. It was vestigial suburbia, everything, in a bag, that she brought with her, though many things she did not pack in her bag came along too.

Jelly Barbarella, he called to her, and she came. She came on so many ships, sailed the fuck in, so many white sails flapping in the cold, dark wind. But what did he know of her? What did she let him know, of her? Diego was an artist, a painter-sculptor, he had grown up on some mean streets, and all his old neighbors were in jail or dead, and he had a motorcycle that he rode with a tiny video camera attached to his helmet sometimes. He told her that it was just part of life, unthinking obligation, instinct, to comment on women. He told her that getting honked at, whistled at, mumbled and muttered indecipherable comments at, should be water off her back. He said that he was upholding a long tradition of the male gaze, not just as an artist, he said, though in what other way he did not say. He said that even what was a response to conventional norms and socially-enforced stereotypes and millennia of misogyny and sexism, was still part of humanity. His father before him was a sculptor, who sculpted tiny men with huge penises.

He invited Stevie to meet his mother when she came to visit. They took a walk around Echo Park Lake. The bougainvillea flowers in the neighborhood were blinding, ruffled by the dry Santa Ana winds, magenta bright sunspots in your eyes. The three of them strolled around the lone fancy home goods boutique. The three of them stood in front of a shelf with minimalist ring dishes spaced evenly apart. Diego's mother ruffled her son's hair. I don't know where he got his face, she said fondly. He doesn't look like me or his father. He looks like an ancient Mayan god with that nose and that mouth, doesn't he? Diego snorted and rolled his eyes, but patted his mother's cheek affectionately and then sauntered outside for a smoke. Diego's mother looped her arm through Stevie's, and then accidentally knocked over a small bowl on display, a considerable portion of it chipping off. While Stevie was expressing her dismay, his mother rotated the bowl and held her finger up to her lips, shhhh, winking at her, and slipped mock-furtively away. Stevie blinked, and walked away too. She did not know that mothers could be like that. She tried to imagine her own mother pushing aside her usual altitudinal sense of righteousness, morality, propriety—pushed aside like a beaded curtain—to act like a teenager. She could not imagine it, could not wrap her golden naïvete around such behavior.

After Stevie and Diego broke up, they broke, were broken—they broke down, really, if you must know—Stevie met James Blackburn Tonville. She loved his super white name. She thought it was wonderful, it could have been aristocratic, it could have been rock and roll, it was Old World sounding, she just thought it was the absolute best, and she would have done anything, changed herself to anyone, in his hands. She felt deserving, of him. Like she had put in her time, after those crazy years with Diego, and now she was intentionally choosing to date James, who was six-feet-two-inches and loved football but also Dvořák and Gerard Manley Hopkins and William Blake and handmaking "ethnic" foods. He and his family, when they got together, conducted prolonged conversations from dinner into the late hours of the night about the states of things like the death penalty and the publishing industry. He was hiiiigh-class.

They lived together in a dark apartment, in West Hollywood. It had carpet, but it was new, Berber carpeting, and there was a front hallway with a tiny half bathroom on the left that she was going to turn into a darkroom. The apartment manager, Timothy, lived in the apartment below them, and they paid him every month by knocking on his door and presenting him with a check, in an envelope, and he answered the door in a heather gray T-shirt and shiny basketball shorts, a buzz cut, boxing matches blaring from his TV. Stevie had a crush on him, wanted to crush him, or be crushed by him. She imagined describing his manner of speaking with the words "drawl" and "laconic."

James had the left side of the closet in their bedroom, and she had the right. He had pushed a dresser into his side, which reminded Stevie of the boys' rooms she had often seen in the model homes she'd toured as a kid with her parents, when they had been looking to move to newer, bigger houses in newer, bigger housing developments. It was the kind of room that's revisited in books and movies by white men in their late thirties who find themselves back in their still-intact childhood bedrooms for one reason or another. Frozen in time, full of habitually dusted trophies and dark wood paneling and hunter green and navy blue, and nonfiction books on history and war, sports team T-shirts and faded hooded sweatshirts.

Stevie met Miles when she was sleeping on an inflatable mattress. She had been hesitant about how long she could sustain a sleeping life with an inflatable—the ostensible reason being that it wasn't the most comfortable sleeping surface, but secretly, she was afraid that it would be the nails to the coffin in her already-so-dormant-as-to-appear-dead sex life post-James Blackburn Tonville. Miles taught her that you can have sex on anything. He seemed to enjoy saying this to her, with his cock inside of her. Later on, even with his cock inside of her—whereas at the beginning, she wouldn't be thinking of anything else, as if his cock, once it penetrated her, expanded, filling up everything, took the shape of the entire inside of her body, spread into the folds of her very brain, in a turgid, turbid, gross way, like the feeling of needing to exhale out your ears—well, later on, even with his cock inside all of her in this way, all she could think about was, well, you're not having sex *on me*. You can't have sex *on* me.

Even then, their sex was not sex. It was Miles having sex with someone inside of her, perhaps a more sexual person. Or was it a less sexual person.

Stevie met Paolo near the bed and breakfast on a terraced vineyard hillside, on the northwestern coast of Italy, in the springtime. He rode on his scooter, around the bend, zooming, but slowly, puttered, tapped a leather shoe on the asphalt, squinted at her, sucked on his cigarette. He didn't say much. Though Stevie liked to remember him as comparable to Nicolas Cage in *Moonstruck*—which, as a kid, she had watched over and over again with her mother—with his mane, his hoarse voice, his dramatically gesturing wooden arm, he was not effusive, like Nicolas Cage, nor did he have a wooden arm. What he did have was unkempt hair and a white undershirt, and a reticence that *could be* masking a deep and fiery love. It took Stevie three days to learn that Paolo had just finished graduate studies in archaeology, that he was expected to take over the inn with his sister, brother-in-law, brother, and "adopted Indian cousin." He had been ending a romance with Lucia, the painter, for the last three years, he told her. She nodded, crossing her arms, sucking on her own cigarette, her sandals making grinding sounds on the gravel in the backyard garden. She thought of the film, *Sex and Lucia*, and the girl in it, riding her bike in a dress only a Mediterranean girl could wear on a bike. She thought of *Lust, Caution*, in which all of the characters were hiding and repressing things, and the secretive women wore a lot of silk and high collars. Sex, Lucia, Lust, Caution, this was the way of the world, as Stevie understood it—everything was about combinations of pairs, everything was about relationships between people and their feelings, everything was about sex, everything was about where you came from, and what you wore while coming.

§

Last year, she was just dating Some Guy. She sometimes refers to him as Some Guy #12, or even #16, even though this is lying. He wanted to see her. A Saturday. Text message. He was brewing beer on his patio. He kissed her. Remember when we had sex outside here on the patio in the fall, he said in her ear. She laughed. She tried to think of something unsentimental and nonchalant to say. Remember when we broke your hammock? she said. This was appropriate to say because surprisingly, they were not trying to have sex on the hammock. They brought the keg inside. She gave him a blowjob, as he stood, leaning back against the wool arm of his wool couch. Fucking wool couch. Nobody wants to touch a wool couch in the summer. He wanted to be able to see her, so she got on her knees. He came in her mouth, and when she paused and moved her mouth away for a second, the rest spurted into the air. Porn-style, exciting. She laughed.

They got up and showered. He set up the hammock. She got up to leave. He told her to try the hammock. She put her purse down, and got in. She decided not to leave. She stayed put. She couldn't move—perfect temperature, perfect breeze, perfect view of green leaves and trees and branches up high, everything disappeared. She didn't even think about how this was all taking place on the patio of some boy's house, some boy she didn't even like all the way, some boy she didn't like enough, to her liking. Some Guy #12. Guy or Boy, which one was a more transparent way to relegate, to deem unimportant? Transparency was very important. Be very clearly this type of girl.

❦

After Some Guy #Something, Stevie got a job opening up American Apparel retail stores. It was Los Angeles, it was the early 2000s, and half of the expressionless models in the AA ads, lamé unitards stretched over baby-fat flesh, were people she knew, and even respected. What were they doing? She stared at their faces. Could she do that? She looked at her own face in the mirror. She wasn't quite sure. She could work managing the stores at least. For a while, she did that. For a while, she did other retail. Her roommate Alyssa works at American Apparel still. Alyssa was recently given the task of driving around and giving out free string bikinis. She got tired and just stuffed them all in her trunk and took a nap in her car. And then she cleaned out her car, and now through their front window, you can see a semi-curtain semi-art installation made out of various solid-colored American Apparel bikini tops.

For a while, Stevie worked in so many restaurants, making so many fancy desserts. For a while, she was a twenty-four-hour diner waitress— her coworkers were a ragtag team of mostly fuck-ups, Z-list actors, and a couple local Thai Town teens. For a while she was a hostess at a fancy corporate restaurant where she made thirty-five bucks an hour to sweetly smile and be the most accommodating, patient, understanding, bright, and serviceable person in the world. She wrote things down on her clipboard so she could find people later, when their tables were ready. Flower shirt. Plaid. Suit. Red hair. Crocs. Board shorts. (This was the westside.) Bald. She shouldn't write bald. Sometimes, people leaned over to look at her clipboard, to check if she had spelled their name correctly, or gotten the number of their party correctly, or just to be nosey. She would gracefully, subtly, shift slightly back, tilting the clipboard away. Even though she was not really hiding anything. She wrote down what time they first checked in with her, so that later, when they claimed they had been waiting for one hour, she could gracefully show them that they were liars.

For the most part she makes very little money in the restaurants. Her eating and sleeping hours are off. She goes out, to everything, at all hours. Everything that is cheap or free. She has started eating food combinations that would have given her eighteen-year-old college self a run for her money. Orange juice in her oatmeal. Not even oatmeal. Just dry instant oats. When she talks to her parents on the phone, and her mother asks her if she's eaten, what has she eaten? Stevie always says, oh, just leftovers.

§

Next, we see Stevie finally emerging out of the cobbling-together-five-restaurant-jobs chrysalis. She has started working at just one restaurant, a Chinese restaurant so that she can meet some Chinese people. Recently, she had a party at her house, and afterwards, someone was like, it was all white people. She blanched. She started working at the restaurant. She has never before in her life had so many ultra Chinese names in her cell phone address book. Ming. Yi Wei. Ling Mei. Lian. Wu Baixi. Sometimes on the train, usually around Pershing Square or on Vermont on the Red Line, when she has no cell phone reception, she will just scroll through her cell phone address book, her eyes catching on these strange letter combinations. Chinese people with Chinese names.

At first, Stevie and Jianpeng, aka Gin, (i.e., My name is Jianpeng, but just call me *Gin*, he said to her with a tough guy look, i.e., Yes, I am the type of guy whose name is a liquor) were just playing in one of the basement-level rooms, a medium-sized storage or electrical supply closet of a room next to the locker room. Last night, he yanked her underwear down over her hips. She was startled. She hadn't seen it coming. They had developed a habit of taking their breaks in this room, with the main overhead lights out, but the room still slightly lit by the hallway lights. They sat at the table in these maroon plastic-cushioned folding chairs, and took turns telling lies, this was his idea. At the beginning, she didn't like it. She had wanted to like it, because it sounded like something cool to like, something cool to be good at, but it went against her instincts, and the layers of it made her full of doubt. When Gin said, I didn't steal five plates, or I once almost killed my best friend in a car accident, Stevie wasn't sure what the truth was. Usually, there wasn't even a clear opposite. I've never masturbated in a restaurant before, he said last night. Stevie said, then, I've never masturbated in front of someone. Which was not right, since this was the truth. She'd simply said the first thing that appeared on her tongue, so that what he had said wouldn't be the last thing hanging in the warm black air, and she hadn't had time to switch it to a lie. And what he did, was this: he hooked the fingers of both hands into the belt loops of her pants, and pulled her over. She went.

They were alone in the restaurant, it wasn't their break after all, it was after they had closed, and everyone else had left, and the two of them were stuck finishing some sidework for the cooks who needed chili peppers cut and string beans cracked, and they were taking a break from that. She straddled him, her foot accidentally catching on his side, and then banging against the table. She knew this was not a good strategy, because once you're straddling someone, there's no way to take your pants off—you only do this if you're wearing a skirt or dress, come on, but he, get this, he grabbed the scissors from the table, the scissors they had been using to cut string beans. At this point, Stevie said, um, because what was he doing. Gin said, honey, that's all he said, and slid a hand behind her neck and up her nape, as if he were a fortuneteller, handling the crystal ball of her head. He could see into her head, and into her future. Probably. Probably, what he saw, as he held her head, was the swarming mess of her life. He moved his hand down, unbuttoned her pants, unzipped, slipped a hand beneath her underwear, and curved his hand around her, holding her, covering her, and then slowly, started snipping at the crotch of her pants with the scissors.

By now, she was squirming, involuntarily pulsing, shifting against his cupped hand, when she heard the metal clank as he placed the scissors back on the table, pulled his hand out, and then used both hands to rip wider the hole in the crotch of her pants. Through the hole, his hand rubbed against the damp fabric of her underwear. Just one inch, that he kept rubbing, back and forth. She wound her arms around his neck, her head fell forward over his shoulder. His other hand held her right buttock, but it wasn't enough, she grabbed it, moved it instead to the front of her tank top, over her breast. She felt him grin against her mouth, she imagined the white of his teeth. She wanted the skin of her neck between those flashing teeth—he slid a knuckle shallowly at the entrance of her pussy—how she was loving that word, when she heard it, it was such a wet and naughty word, taut—and how it felt was glossy. A glossy photograph, a streak, translucent pectin covering a fruit-covered tart. He held his knuckle up to her face. It smelled, she guessed; then he suddenly pushed her off him, stood up, nudged the tip of his penis to her right nostril. It felt soft, like a baby's elbow, blindly moving about, wildly, scrabbling, getting into trouble. You cannot smell this? He demanded, in his contraction-less English.

This occurrence was entirely confusing to her. He was Chinese, wasn't that meaningful? She only felt disoriented—the meaning, if it was out there floating somewhere, was definitely beyond her grasp. She went home and sat at the small table in the kitchen. She lay her right cheek down on the cool, hard surface of the formica tabletop. She felt it, felt shaken up. But why? She was used to having sex in restaurants after hours, with chefs, mainly, who all blurred together in her mind into a softened butter batter of thick, scarred forearms, pierced penises, and neck and chest tattoos. That last one in Santa Monica, had been an ex-frat bro, the surfer California kind, and he had liked to stick his finger into raw mixtures of things in the kitchen and then stick it into her ear.

It was always a bunch of miscreants working in restaurants, herself included, she thought. She thought to herself, I am out of control. What was she even saying, *used to having sex in restaurants*. What was she even doing here? She had promised herself she wouldn't work in restaurants anymore. Or, she had at least thought about it. This was what happened in restaurants. Sex messes. She had to get out of it. Get it together. Get something normal, proper, going for herself.

Since leaving California behind, since California-deserting, since moving to New York, Stevie has taken on a new shape. She has left behind the part of her life that is messy, and is now on a newfound, mess-free streak of life. There are many ways in which she can see that she has come a long way. There are many ways in which the negative space surrounding the shape of her life is now gaining a newfound clarity, a boldly defined outline. She doesn't need strictly enforced rules, because things are just kind of falling into place, in a very natural way. She doesn't even make her bed every morning, at least not well. But it is all working out, because it is all about priorities. She doesn't live in a home, much less a city, that is cockroach-free. But she does have a non-restaurant job, working in a semi-respectable office, doing copyediting.

Speaking of coming a long way, Stevie met a golden boy last month. She met Dave at a party. This is something they both do, she and him, go to parties. This is something that goes in the middle of the Venn diagram of the two of them. His hair, it is made of gold, soft. His smile is big, easy, like a wedge of hard fresh cheese. Everything about him walks the line of good, not mediocre, not pretty good, not so-so, not great, not extraordinary, but the solid hard line of good. He is smart, in a *good* way. He is funny, and witty, in a *good* way. He is interested in *good* things: sustainable living and the environment, traveling, non-profit work, playing his guitar, photography, scuba diving, hiking, rock climbing, frisbee, Buddhism. He drinks and smokes pot, in a *good* way, gave up cigarettes two years ago. His aura, it is golden boy gold.

It is good for her, that she has found a golden boy. Yesterday, away from the golden boy, she spent the day walking around the city aimlessly connecting checklist dots. This is the coffee shop she goes to, on blank days like this, so she made her way over, had her coffee outside on a bench in the sun. The bench tilted forward, it was difficult to sit without feeling like falling. She stood up and walked to the train, took the train across the bridge, walked to the doughnut shop, had a doughnut on another bench, on a parkway. She stopped by the bookstore that she usually stops by, if in the area, and then continued walking north. She walked west, to the park, and sat in the dry fountain, until the sun slid below the skyline. She sat on another bench in the park, finished her doughnut, and then slowly made her way home.

Yesterday, away from the golden boy, Stevie had a temporary lapse in the evening, spent hours smoking cigarettes with her roommate Conor, alternating between sending each other further into their respective bouts of depression, and making attempts to advise and uplift and encourage. Stevie thought she had left all the mess of her last life behind, but at any moment, it could get messy again. And Conor—he was totally a mess. Their lives were messes, and they were swimming in them, barely wading, drowning in manic words. She stood in her doorway, she leaned against the kitchen counter, she fixed them some eggs and ham and cheese on toast, they crouched in the wind on the roof trying to light their smokes.

While this was going down, downward, the golden boy was at a birthday party. He had spent the day helping his best-friend-*slash*-business-partner move into a new apartment. He was then moving on to doing other things that did not involve losing your shit and getting your shit together and throwing things and not being able to do it and never being able to do things and unhappiness and general mania and crouching in the wind on the roof.

She goes to the golden boy's apartment in downtown Brooklyn on Saturday afternoon. She asks him about his family, about his undergraduate thesis, for which he spent summers researching tadpoles in the salt marshes of Rhode Island. She pictures herself spending next Thanksgiving at his parents' house, a very model-home-, storybook-type of house. She puts her first name together with his last name, even though she is not the type of girl to ever get married, much less take her hypothetical husband's last name. They sit at his breakfast nook, warm, white sunlight pouring in through the windows. They eat huevos rancheros off matching pale green plates, forks clinking on ceramic. They pause between mouthfuls to grin at each other. He reaches over to smooth back her hair. Instead of squinting joke-suspiciously at him, she smiles winningly.

&

On the morning of The Morning, the golden boy says to Stevie, did you read the book I...? Gave, you, the Zen one—those words would come next, one after another. Recently, Stevie has started to think, why bother in this life, to finish all these sentences, aren't half of the sentences you say only half necessary, don't you already know what words come next, wasted breath, wasted words, wasted time and this signal that you are only finishing what you started for the sake of finishing what you started? This is when you're in trouble, when it's not working anymore, when the decline has started, how it starts, with a few piddling degrees of a decline.

As he tests her, the golden boy is waiting for his bread to spring out of the toaster. They have been living together for almost a year now. When they moved in together, he wanted to get a toaster that looked like a toaster, and Stevie wanted a toaster oven, which looks like an oven. It is hard to win, against a golden boy. The golden boy, he stands still as a statue. He is an Oscar statuette, all smooth hard curves. Nothing can get to him. Even without moving, he seemed to press forward, gently push her back. She swallowed, and backed against the kitchen counter, hit her back, had nowhere left to back. He had interests, *interests*, in the traditionality of waiting for toast, which is only rewarded—happiness, completion—only rewarded, by the springing ping of the toast popping up out of its slots. Rituals, triggers, traditions. Catalysts for catalysts.

Once, at the beginning, before there were things like toasters sitting in between them, Stevie had thought they were more fitting. There was some complacent sense to this, once, a sense sculpted out of strange but insistent pathways in her thought. She was a golden girl with him, once, a girl made of sand, lifted from the southern California desert. She thought, once, how beautiful they would be together, why yes, why, yes, they would always have that beauty at least, the sensible beauty of a golden boy and a golden girl, pieced together into a terrifically golden bursting glow.

I'm sorry, the golden boy said, finally, once they were already out in his car. It was the final moment, Stevie felt sure of it, that all there was of them, had been of them, had been leading to this, the terrible notion that now that you know the ending, there were so many nodes and notches along the way up, along the way down, that you could have grabbed at, that you could have taken to twist this into something else, to wring something, anything, other than this, out of this sopping soaking mess. To have squeezed hard, long, in anticipation of one last drop, and have the last drop be this?

They sat hard, they sat so so hard, she thought maybe she would be ground into the seat, never leave, they would be immobilized and immortalized in this space, each staring straight ahead, out of the front windshield of his small green hatchback. The golden boy did not believe in apologies, so why was he even saying sorry? They had fought about this before, how to express sorrow then, how to take responsibility, how to begin to make amends, how to demonstrate remorse and sympathy? The golden boy, on his way to the gym, on his way to the rock-climbing wall, on his way out the door, did not even shake his golden curled head, would look affrontedly into Stevie's eyes, would tenderly smooth back her hair, would readjust the shoulder strap on his gym bag, and would say, you work harder, to lead a cleaner life, one that doesn't allow for the option of apology.

Can you make out the shape of Stevie? Can Stevie make it out? She wanted, at least, to make out the shape of the story, to be able to tell the story of her broken heart. Once, a golden boy broke her heart. He used the word "trampled" once, and so she uses it too now at the 38th Street Diner, for continuity, for a semblance of levity, for distance. Who? Some dude, she said. She has said this so many times. Some guy, some boy, some dude, some *dude*, she says. Tired, impatient. If it was broken once, it's proof that it exists, she had one, she has one, even if it's shapeless now. Trampled. Broken. Glass, shards, drops of blood. Shreds of flesh, a shredded chicken salad, cold, unappetizing.

But, she finds that she wants to say these things, these words: heart, break, once. She wants to have lived it. She wants to have been alive enough. She wants to have held something out, some *thing*, held out like an offering in her palm, a true bloody story, held out like a blood-soaked sock. In such a story, Stevie wonders, when does the girl get to turn into something else, instead of the end-all being a slender and pure white princess? When does the transformation of the girl into a beast, a predator, something dangerous and fierce, vicious and sharp-edged, get to be not just a turning point, but the storybook ending? When does the girl get to be a great white shark, a crocodile, a wolf, a fox, a grizzly bear, a tiger, forever, not ever wishing to be something less messy? Stevie thinks she will say these things: break, tear apart, blood. She could do it, she could strike fear, into the soft pulsating hearts of golden boys and golden girls, everywhere.

Her old friend, her old roommate, Alyssa, moved recently to Philly, and Stevie convinced her to come to New York for a visit. Sitting there in the diner, she looks across the table at Alyssa who is looking down at the menu. There is scaffolding outside, and this scaffolding has clung to this building for a very long time. She thinks of it less as scaffolding, and more as a symbiotic relationship: scaffold and diner. This is the vaguely optimistic way of putting it, instead of putting it the other way—like the relationship between her mother and her father, who have the opposite of a symbiotic relationship, a relationship in which both entities suffer a net loss. But, like the scaffold and diner, her parents' relationship has existed in this fashion for too long to change. And yet when Stevie was twenty-seven, her mother told her it wasn't too late, that she could still become an architect. She had looked at her mother then, and felt sorry for her. Perhaps her mother was not completely wrong though, perhaps there is not actually anything in her own life that has existed for so long that it is too late to change.

When Stevie is done with her story, Alyssa scoots out of the booth to go use the restroom in the back. When she returns, as she is sliding back into the booth, Stevie makes sure that she is busy doing something, so she shakes some drops of Tabasco sauce on top of her pile of scrambled eggs. Then she works on arranging a very even pile of the eggs onto the wedge of toast she has left, and every time one curd or crumble of egg falls off, she carefully places it back on the pile until the shape holds completely steady.

The Closing Doors

OFF VESTAL AVENUE, the front door of the bungalow had a glass pane bisecting the heavy wood. There was yellow light inside, a warm chorus of voices, transforming, and then transforming again. Inside, the woman walked directly to the table with food, looked at the table only, and not at anyone's eyes. She did not say hello, or touch, anyone. There was already a man at the table—a man with a neutral look, unstyled pants, unstyled hair, a most regular T-shirt and running shoes. He was eating shrimp cocktail, a ring of them, plump, arched flesh.

He looked at her, the shrimp, her shoulder, her body. The woman pretended not to see that, because she wasn't sure she saw it, and instead smiled vaguely in his direction, politely, and looked over the party snacks laid out on the vinyl blue tablecloth. The orange cubes of cheese had taken on a plastic oxygenated coating. The woman sucked her teeth. She wanted shrimp cocktail but the man now had the entire black plastic tray in his hand. Perhaps he had brought it himself, for himself, a personal party snack.

Hello, the man said. He lifted his body from the wall he was leaning against, and straightened himself, without moving any closer. The woman put her hand out in the emptiness between them, and said, Hello. She looked at him now, his face, his blue eyes, that were looking away. They looked away, but then not. She realized one eye was a lazy eye. She realized this in a way in which something moved inside her body, a flip, or click, but nothing moved outside. Outside, she was unmoved, gave nothing away, was smooth, like the tender and opaque skin of a silkworm. She observed the lazy blue-blood eye, in an otherwise very symmetrical, geometrical profile. The shapes of his face were angular, like the handsome weatherman she watched, with the sound off, in her underwear on weekday evenings.

The man moved over to stand next to the woman. By not moving, she was choosing to be close to someone. His body stood very near her body, and he thrust his tray of cocktail shrimp toward her, pushing it just to her breasts. She didn't know if he could see what he had done with those eyes—she had no idea what it looked like, the world, seen or not seen from those eyes—but surely he could feel that the tray had hit up against her flesh. He didn't move. She pressed closer. It was her, the tray of shrimp, and the man with the lazy eye. He didn't move back. He grinned at her, with his teeth, but his eye stayed cool, aloof. She picked up a shrimp, its cold plasticky tail, dipped its head end, headless now, deliberately into the red sauce in the bowl in the center of the ring. The shrimp had a cold, sweet, ocean taste. Her teeth sinking into its soft cartilage crunch, the woman felt opened, a memory of the first glimpse of a blue wedge of sea in the distance, after a long drive from the Inland Empire, toward the empty tangle of California coast.

What's your story, the man asked, his cool blue eye looking just slightly off, uninterested. It was so slight almost as to seem a figment. The woman was good at angles and spatial judgment and playing pool, though, and she knew that if she drew a sightline from one eye and then the other, the lines would not be parallel. At some point off in the distance—who knew when, but what did it matter when if it was inevitable—they would intersect. They were imperfect.

I'm a cousin of a boyfriend of a sister of the roommate of the friend's boss. The woman said this, and then looked straight at the lazy eye. The lazy eye looked back at her, the jokey her. Chameleons did that, had eyes that went different places. But on purpose, they had control.

Yeah, huh, he said. She looked away, down at a book on the table. It had a clear, plastic protective covering, over a hard, tan cover.

It's the Bible, he said, in French.

Why are you reading the Bible at a party? she asked, in French.

To meet women, he responded, leaning back against the wall. His lazy eye winked. She saw it, she didn't see it. She was beginning to feel anxious, her blood beating a course at random. She moved slightly away from him. She hoped not to wake him up to the fact that she was moving. Then she turned her back on him entirely and moved further away. She walked into the next room with a forward-moving intention, as if she were progressing through the logic of a haunted house. There were things to see, next steps, things you were not allowed to leave without experiencing. Room after room after room, and then, somehow, she seemed to be back at the first room. The man with the lazy eye stood in place, looking the other way.

The woman sat down at one of the chairs next to the table. Most of the party had moved now to the living room in the back, and the patio. There were Marcel Dzama prints lined up on the white walls near the man's head, of trees and people-trees, and branch-arms. Blank-faced people. Frozen-in-dance people. The man was still holding the tray of shrimp cocktail, maybe looking away, at the distance over her shoulder. The party moved back in a wave, a crowd of people pushing into her train car, even when the doors were trying to close. Good thing she had found a seat. She looped an arm through the straps of her purse, which sat unevenly on her lap. It was heavy, there was an odd angle near the top, from a book she had inside, which was not the Bible. It was a copy of *The Passionfruit Flower* that she had stuffed in at the last minute, in case of emergency. *Stand clear of the closing doors please*, the pre-recorded voice intoned druggily over the subway speakers, and the doors pushed shut. People shifted, bodies accommodating bodies, until each one was evenly spaced apart. The woman finally lifted her eyes.

There was a new man standing in front of her—she was eye-level with his crotch. He was wearing jeans fitted enough that she could see the protuberance of his penis, slanted slightly to the right. She swallowed, feeling sick, altitudinal. She looked to the left. There was a red-looking man, spilling out liquidly from his clothing, bulbous and drunk. The heat in the car was on very, very high. The woman slid a hand into the front of her shirt, and over her shoulder, to massage the back of her neck, sweating. The girl standing next to the man in front of her had on a baggy coat, and a scarf, which when she readjusted, revealed that inside, all she wore was an open-work lace and mesh top, and an operatic black bra. She had on a long gray billowy skirt, and no makeup. Sad eyes. Full lips. The woman looked back, deliberately at the man's penis, imagining it under the denim. It was there. Her face was less than fifteen inches away from it. She thought she saw it move. She looked up, but the man's face was blocked by the newspaper he was reading. All she had to go by was this.

The woman looked around for something familiar, found it. The MTA New York City Subway map. She stared at the map, at the curved hanging penis shape of Manhattan, looked carefully, looked again. She was overcome with the desire to impale herself on it. It looked about the right size, the perfect size, on the map, just wide and thick enough to penetrate her every wall, dully heavy against every surface. Once she got that thing, that shape, inside of her, there would be no room for anything else. She would only feel the throb of 1.6 million people coursing through her. And what were those tiny protrusions, tiny piers sticking out the side of the southwest of the island? She could feel them press, like so many rough fingertips, dragging against her swollen vagina. She pulled the collar of her V-neck T-shirt down, down over her naked breast, bare, there. She stood among the throng, turned feverishly to the poster, pressed her nipple against the cock that was Manhattan. It was warm. It was hard. Of course it was hard, it was covered in plastic.

She felt something brush by her head. She looked up. The man had lowered his newspaper. *Le Figaro.* He had glossy combed hair, a blind-brown mustache and beard. Both of his eyes looked straight at her, and saw just her version of her. If they were parallel laser beam sightlines—he would only be able to kill off people coming from one direction. She felt deprived. He blinked his dark lashes at her, once, twice. He blinked his pale naked mouth, full lips touching, not touching. She swallowed, it wasn't until she had to swallow that she realized she hadn't completely closed her mouth. The girl in the lace shirt stared down impassively, both eyes. Her breasts were perfect, paper white, delicately turgid. The man shifted his stance. The woman wondered what still surface she might be disturbing if she reached up and touched him. She lifted her hand, lightly brushed her fingertips over the front of the man's jeans. She did not care, did not even wait to look at the reaction or response. She groaned a little, by accident, feeling as if she had wet her own pants. The feeling was, was that once her vagina had been covered, held in place by something, and now, something had fallen away so suddenly, been yanked out so completely, leaving there a nestled, pulsating animal, and there was something else that needed to go there, fast. She looked up, to see the man shifting closer. In one motion, one moment, she stood up, and the train car emptied.

Only the man with the lazy blue eye was left. The woman took the tray of shrimp cocktail from his hand and placed it on the table, on top of the Bible. They walked to the bathroom down the hallway by the kitchen. Inside the bathroom, he pulled down her pants and underwear together, lifted her by her waist onto the bathroom counter by the sink. She opened her legs, mouth watering, vagina watering. He got down on his knees, and the woman thought he was going to push his tongue in her, but instead, he parted her thighs further with his hands, and put his eyes to her. She imagined his lazy blue eye, slightly off, looking very exploratory and renegade. She could feel him seeing her, through her soaking cunt. That was probably part of it, you could probably see more, and more easily, the wetter you were. She didn't care what he saw, that he could probably see everything she had ever hated about herself. She wanted to stick him inside her, his whole self. Starting with his cock, which she was reaching for. It was a hot, sticky world inside those pants. The woman couldn't wait, was dying for that first penetration, she was wet, but further, deeper inside, and first, as she pulled the tip of his penis inside her, it rubbed, sticking, full of friction, resistance, like rubbing two erasers together. But she could feel the dripping, the coating, that waited further in, and, Hey, he said, easy. She liked that, that he said this, as if she was out of control. She was out of control. She would swallow him whole, down there. He would come out the other end a moth, dusty paper wings fluttering from her mouth, a gray powder left on her lips.

I See My Eye In Your Eye

1990

THERE IS THE DRY heat of August, and there are the two of us, pushing lightly through it. My sister and I are eleven and nine. Our mother is taking us on our annual visit to Dr. Chinn, the eye doctor, to *kàn yǎnjīng*—see the eye.

Hailey and I dread seeing our eyes. She says nothing to me, but I assume it must be the same for her as it is for me, because we are sisters and this is how it is for us. The visits are excruciatingly shameful horror-shows, as we dig our own graves with our halting recitation of the letters and numbers. Then comes that small sheet of paper, torn off a pad. The new prescription is concrete evidence that our eyesight has deteriorated yet again. I eat dozens of baby carrots in the week leading up to our appointment. But there is no hope, not really.

The sallow-skinned teenage receptionist is a cousin or niece of the Chinns, forced to work there for free during her summer vacations. She asks politely, in perfectly enunciated Mandarin, "Would your mother like to go in with you?" I look back at my mother, hoping that for once she might let us go in by ourselves. But she always follows us in, sits on the bland mauve chair, crosses her ankles, presses her lips into a tight horizontal line, watching us as we stumble over our Es and 3s and Fs and Bs. The eye chart moves further and further away and becomes a rapidly escaping, glowing blur. Everything inside my quiet nine-year-old body starts to twist and furl, compressing itself into a tight foil ball sitting inert in my abdomen. When I struggle, my mother presses her lips even tighter, and then tightly announces that we shouldn't be reading so many books. I dread this pronouncement every year. All I have are books. We walk out of the medical plaza, seemingly hours later, the sun white, the buildings blinding, my eyes feeling sorry for themselves. But at least we are free until next summer.

1995

Hailey is sixteen and I am fourteen, and I am in eighth grade. The first two weeks of health class have been reserved for sex ed. This phrase, *sex ed*, has been sprinkled into our middle school conversations, with a feeling similar to the tentative first uses of swear words, forbidden and sweet. Our homework assignment is to find an empty box, wrap it in wrapping paper, tie a bow on it, make it nice, and bring it in. On Monday afternoon in fifth period, Ms. Kruger explains the significance: these gift-wrapped boxes are ours to keep and treasure, because our virginity is a gift that can only be given once. It must be kept intact for the perfect person who will receive our gift. She keeps repeating that word, *gift*.

At the end of class, to review the various genital parts and functions we had learned about the Friday before, Ms. Kruger calls me up to the paper cutouts taped on the whiteboard in front of the room. "Make the penis erect," she orders. I have no idea what I'm doing, but I shift the paper penis on its brass paper-fastener axis, and make it perpendicular. "More," she says. I move it again. It swings back down. Nobody makes a sound. I clench my teeth, smile to nobody in particular, sit back down.

My mother got upset at me the afternoon before, when I hadn't been able to explain why I was wasting so much of her wrapping paper and ribbon. The only box I had been able to find to wrap was a really big one, the box the vacuum cleaner came in. My sister snickered from the family room coffee table where she was spread out doing homework. My mother had left the kitchen where she had been busy preparing dinner, washing something, chopping something with the big rectangular Chinese knife on the big white cutting board. She stood in the middle of the living room and sounded stricken, while I sat on the ground in front of the hall closet, wrapping paper everywhere. I ran upstairs and tried to slam my bedroom door—even though it had been designed to be slam-proof—and in my head angrily did direct literal translations of things my mother said in Chinese into English. *"Are you wanting to harm me to death?!"* It made her sound stupid.

1996

Hailey is seventeen, I am fifteen. We are in high school when the storm hits. *El Niño.* The boy. It hits some of my girlfriends like a cartoon punch in the stomach, a stampede of boy-craziness. Hordes of boys. Everyone else is blooming, flowers everywhere, the sky dusty with pollen. People can't see. I keep my head down, my throat back, mouth in perpetual laughter, as my eyes watch it pass me by.

I am late to the party. A "late bloomer," I decide later. But for now, I am tortured, scarred from being barred from sleepover parties in elementary school because a number of my friends' parents were divorced. "You can't trust that," my parents had countered. "Who knows what strangers might be in their homes? New boyfriends, new girlfriends..." They considered this explanation an act of generosity. They weren't under any obligation to provide me with an explanation—they were my parents.

1997

Hailey is eighteen, and I am sixteen, and we are feeling it. We are trapped in Orange County, where suburbs mean rich and safe and uniform, not like the *banlieues* of Paris. In French class, Madame Vaillant smuggles in a copy of *La Haine* from her sister, a professor in the film and television department at USC. Madame's graying feathered hair sways back and forth as she vehemently paces around the classroom. She wants us to see what Paris is really like. She wants to dispel all the romantic notions we had that made us want to take French in the first place. "This is the *real* France," she says, jabbing the top of the A/V cart. I leave class on Friday repeating aggressive phrases of French slang in my head. *Quoi! N'importe quoi! De quoi tu parles?! Je m'en fou! Ferme ta guele!*

1999

We are twenty and eighteen now, my sister and I. Along with our mother, we are making our annual summer pilgrimage back to Dr. Chinn's office. We still make our appointments together after all these years, and always in August, in the clean, shimmery heat of the Orange County summer. The only difference is that now my sister drives the station wagon instead while my mother rides shotgun. On the way there, I think about the eye chart. What font was that anyway? An ugly one. Though I can make spot-on judgments about the typeface and kerning, the receptionist is still a desperate-looking Chinese teen who speaks perfect Chinese. She makes me feel angry—at her, at myself.

People look up as we enter the waiting room. They probably look up every time the door opens, but I imagine they stare longer at us because they are not used to seeing Asian kids like my sister and me: hot pink hair, camo pants, baseball tee that says 'Label Whore' (my sister), lightning bolt shaved into the right side of my head, hippie dress, and cowboy boots (me), and tattoos (both of us). I have never wondered about this before, how it must be for my mother to have the two of us as daughters in a town like this, two Chinese girls, who, while arguably obedient and well-behaved and polite enough, only care about literature and art and food and far-away places. In a town like this, the norm consisted of all the Asians and Jews and Persians and fifth-generation USC WASPs alike, climbing and clambering over each other in piles of straitlaced limbs, racing to become surgeons and corporate lawyers and masters of money.

My sister and I have carefully cultivated low-culture tastes in order to balance out all those summer family vacations traipsing around Monet's garden and the Burgundy wine region and the British Museum. I like Led Zeppelin, donuts, trashy romance novels, and monster truck rallies. Despite the inconvenience of my Chinese-ness, this basically makes me white trash in a place like Orange County. Or rather, as my sister writes in a Berkeley sociology class paper, "These second-generation immigrants are proto-western aliens: their survivor-class parents winnowing down into striver-class offspring, cultivated in a family dynamic that is pressurized by overachievement and suburban stasis. When these suburbanite children masquerade as white-trash wannabes in the big cities, they are defiantly enacting—performing, even—a sublimation of their parents' upper-middle-class dreams." Ta-dah! I find this very impressive at the time.

2004

"Mom says I have to go to the dentist," Hailey is saying as we drive up the 110 toward Highland Park. She is twenty-five and I am twenty-three. We have managed to escape from the first obligation of the evening—a summer fundraiser party put on by the organization where Hailey works. We took advantage of the complimentary dessert buffet. We watched Young Hollywood and CAA agents and their assistants mingling their fucking hearts out. They were having the time of their lives in high heels.

Hailey starts opening and closing her mouth, testing her jaw. "My jaw makes a weird clicking sound. Does yours do that?" She keeps jawing the air, brings a hand up to her jawline. "I don't know, I think it might be because I used to grind my teeth. But mom says I might get lockjaw." "Really?" I say, only half paying attention. Lockjaw seems kind of extreme. "I can hear that," I inform her. "What?" "Your jaw." "Oh, shit, really? You can hear that?" She resumes clicking her jaw. "Yup," I say, turning back to look out the window. "Too many blowjobs," she says, suddenly. "Ha," I say. "That's ridiculous." "Think so?" she laughs. I shrug, and resume my survey of the passing scenery outside the window, the gas stations and pool halls.

There are certain points in my life when I am sure that I'm not supposed to be doing what I am actually doing. Riding in the car with my sister after leaving some benefit to go play pool in Highland Park is something I probably *am* supposed to be doing. But last Thursday evening, I was the only person still working late in the office, for the tenth night in a row, and I was stabbing at my two-day-old leftover apple pear coleslaw and cold bacon lunch with a plastic fork, instead of at a gross, whisky-sodden party on Temple, where everyone else in the world was.

Was. But I kept stabbing at the julienned fruit, skirting the curls of limp bacon.

I don't think I am supposed to be doing that, doing this. These days, these office hours, these smiles that appear and disappear, they carve the thinnest, most delicate of slices, a peeler skinning a mango. After the skin, I start peeling the fibrous yellow-orange flesh juicily away, and now I am skinning off pieces of the heart, sunny-squawking-toucan-yellow-orange pieces, and the tangy sweetness folds, pales, shrinks, disappears.

I wish I were a snake. Rubbing, rubbing at my neck, rubbing until my entire body of skin, a skinsuit, rubs off in one piece, a one-piece skinsuit. I would shed, molt, all the fucking time. Get the shit out of my skin, *get the hell out of Dodge.*

Hailey and I get to the bar. There are a lot of mountain-men-looking guys there—long hair, beards, plaid shirts—and some Latino guys who look straight out of *Wassup Rockers.* I have a brief run-in with my friend, Freddie, who is always texting me, "Noodles." "Noodles??" "Noodles!!" Sometimes spelled wrong: "Nooddles!" "Nodoles!" perhaps in the throes of hunger. After I say hi to Freddie, Hailey and I play pool with a couple of the rocker guys—one is Mexican, and the other Filipino—and then we go with them out front to smoke a joint. They have locked their fixies out front. One of them works as a bike courier downtown. They rhapsodize about bicycles. Hailey and I laugh at the same time, out of nowhere and for nothing. The two boys, Johnny and Ruben, grew up in Highland Park.

Johnny is saying, "...yo, those white guys walk around this neighborhood and they're not scared at all! And me? I've lived here all my life! And I walk around, and I'm scared. Why am I scared when these white kids aren't scared?" Hailey and I wait for the answer, wait for it... "Well, it's because they're white. Nobody will bother white kids. And if they do get bothered, cops would take notice. People would care." Hailey and I nod. "Do they bother Chinese people?" we ask. They shrug. "No, probably not." My sister and I look at each other. Then we leave them to go get tacos.

2007

My sister and I are twenty-eight and twenty-six now, and the Hailey-and-Peter-Blackburn engagement after-party is at Peter Blackburn's apartment on Lanterman Terrace. The narrow apartment balcony looks out onto a squash court, seemingly squeezed into a very odd courtyard space in the middle of apartment buildings and dark palms. On the other side of the buildings, I can see lights over by the L.A. River. Here, though, there is only a single light shooting vacantly down on the empty court.

I turn back around to look through the sliding glass door. My sister is still explaining the rules of Taboo to the uninitiated. I haven't seen her in about four months. She looks thinner. I glance over at Peter, watch as he teasingly slaps Hailey on the thigh. I look back down at my whiskey. They are in love. Hailey is marrying this guy at his family's estate in the Hamptons next spring, and then they are moving to Chicago to attend business school together. This is a legitimate life she is taking on.

Usually, I watch Hailey, and decide either to do the same or the exact opposite. Looking back down at my drink, I am blindsided by the notion that I don't know how I feel about this new legitimacy. I don't know if it makes me want to cry or throw up.

I look up. "Where have you been all week," Dieter asks impatiently, possessively, and I can feel it, can feel myself liking it, so I frown. I slide him a brief glance which is all I have to spare, and then look away. "Chinatown," I say. He doesn't say anything but continues to look at me. "A couple art show openings," I say, as if I go to openings all the time. I shift my glance casually back to him. "How's it going?" "Good," he says, but there is a layer or edge of something, in how he says it. We walk around to the other side of the balcony and down the stairs, so that we are standing on the cliff of one of the hills outside Peter Blackburn's place.

"For a city with so many holes, L.A. sure is impenetrable," he remarks, nodding out toward the open valley below. There is smoke streaming out his mouth as he exhales in the dark. I wonder if he is trying to say something big, maybe something about me. Below: the lights of Frogtown, the empty black strip of the river, Cypress Park, Mount Washington. Lights, lots of them, but tiny pinpricked points.

Back inside, Hailey waves me over to where she is sitting on a brown leather sectional sofa. "Remember when James and I broke up, you cried?" she says. I hold still for a moment, helpless to the feeling of alcohol in my blood, before I remember that this is true. She does this sometimes, brings up incidents that happened long ago, incidents that I have forgotten. Usually it involves me crying.

"I totally forgot about that," I say, kind of smiling. "I don't know. I was really shocked. I thought that was it. I thought you guys would be together forever." James was her first boyfriend. We had all gone to the same elementary school, middle school, high school, college. He had lived only three blocks away from us. But he was the star lacrosse player in high school, which made him seem far, far away.

"Yeah, well," she says. She flicks her cigarette at the black block-shaped ashtray on the table, and looks over at Peter who is standing on one foot and making kicking motions on the other side of the room. "It's not ever the end of the world," she says, "not even love or the end of love. None of it." She turns back toward me, looks in my eye as if challenging me to take up my usual position on this, contrary to hers. As children, she liked purple, I liked pink. She liked turkey, I liked ham. She liked American cheese, I liked Swiss. I try to pull an exasperated expression over my face, but find myself glancing over at Dieter. I feel suddenly cold, a soreness in my throat.

"Let's try to do something this weekend," I say. I look back at Hailey; she looks surprised. I am not known for saying things like this out loud.

Dieter and I get back to my place around two a.m., and we share my microwaved leftovers from Chung King. We decide it would be the best idea ever to take a ride on his motorcycle, despite the fact that he's drunk, despite the fact that his bike has been unreliable for the past two months. Three weeks ago, I had to pick him up off the side of the 101 freeway on-ramp and help him push the gleaming, recalcitrant thing to the side, so that he could go home and get a part, and then go back and patch something up so that he could ride it all the way to the shop.

Reasons not to go on the ride are overshadowed by our drunken enthusiasm, and we grab at helmets, pull on boots. I send Hailey a text message as Dieter guides the bike backwards down the driveway, something about having lunch over the weekend, just so I'll have said something to someone. Just in case something happens, I'll have said something. Dieter and I decide we want somewhere scary—*a cemetery!*—we shout at the same time. He wants to go to East L.A., where there is a cemetery his coworker talks about a lot. It's off the 60, never mind why his coworker would be talking about any cemetery a lot. I rack my swimmy brain for other, more viable cemeteries, throw out the one in Westwood off Veteran, the one on Venice Blvd across from Loyola High. We decide the closest one is Hollywood Forever, but after a blur of a ride that feels supremely long, a ride that in reality must only have taken ten or fifteen minutes, we come upon barricades and cops blocking the cemetery gates. So we turn around, and try to get to the old L.A. Zoo ruins at Griffith Park. But everything is barricaded, blocked off, gates down, closed. Everything fails. Even in my ruffled teal skirt, we fail.

We make it back to my house, through the warm, windy darkness. So we sit back down on the couch, in a post-drunk, pre-hangover haze, and talk about this thing we have been talking about, a marriage of convenience.

He gets his laptop out and starts looking up procedures and laws and bylaws on EU citizenship and EU work visas. I kick myself for not having taken German in high school instead of French, even though at one point I had already kicked myself for not having taken Spanish instead. Hailey texts me back about meeting up on Sunday. Dieter and I argue about whether or not it would be a good idea for me to tell Hailey—Hailey who really is not the biggest fan of Dieter—about our upcoming nuptials. *Nuptials!* We cannot stop saying this word—oh man, our nuptials—they are fucking... *impending!* and how I will convince my parents I want to move to Europe when they think I should move to China. We fall asleep on the couch like that, laptop in his lap, phone in my hand.

2009

My sister is thirty, I am twenty-eight. I'm stuck by myself this time, with my parents. How did this happen?

"We didn't ask that much of you," my parents are saying. They don't sit next to each other in the booth. "We didn't make you be doctors," they say. "We didn't even make you marry doctors." These have been half jokes my entire life.

"Do you know," I begin, "I just realized yesterday that I've only ever attended one wedding without the two of you?"

My parents look confused. "So?"

"So? That's sad," I say.

"No it's not," my mom says. "It just means your friends haven't really started getting married yet."

"But why?" I ask, listlessly, rhetorically.

"Why haven't *you* decided to get married?" she asks.

I roll my eyes, "I don't want to."

"Yes," she says, "because you're not ready to lose your freedom yet. And so you're friends with people who are just like you, who also are not ready. Yet. You all know that once you get married, you lose your freedom."

"Yeah, well," I reply, "just remember you said that. And don't be surprised or upset when I decide that I don't ever want to get married."

She inhales, "You've decided that? Your dad would certainly be upset." I don't look up to see what my dad's expression is. I am trying to enjoy my dinner. Shredded pork and bean curd, hollow-hearted greens, ants crawling up a tree. I am trying to not listen. For the rest of the dinner, I open my mouth only to blast hot solid rectangular prisms of aggressive silence.

This is how I know I'm older, because people start saying these things. As if it's ever appropriate to tell someone they should consider settling down. Settling down is what pilgrims and pioneers do. What school teachers tell their unruly pupils to do. In the car later, my mother brings it up again.

"You should still consider settling down."

"I don't have time," I say vaguely, to bide myself some time.

"Don't have time?" she asks, "You don't have time to find someone, or you don't have time for the kind of life your sister has, with a baby and a husband?"

"Both," I say, again trying to hand over only the broadest, nothingest answers I can produce. I change my mind. "No, that's not right," I say, "I don't really *not* have time. I just don't have the desire."

"That's because you haven't decided you're ready to lose your freedom yet," she says, triumphantly, as if we have made a true breakthrough, as if we have struck gold. I nod, as if I believe the same.

In front, my dad's mouth is in the shape of a soft, blurry smile. I think that he must be remembering a joke, one that takes place in a distant land.

I am 29.

Two roads. One is straight, a logical continuation. The other one? Weird. I shouldn't take it. It doesn't make sense. It's going the wrong way. It's going backwards. It *is* backwards. But I guess I've taken it. This other one.

&

On an empty Sunday afternoon, I find myself driving down Pacific Coast Highway, near Malibu. The sun is hitting a path through to the horizon, and the surface of the sea blinks clear-eyed points of light over the opaque grayness of the water. A smattering of wetsuit-skinned surfers' backs, bobbing, facing something I cannot see. Before me are road trip clouds stretching to the very edge of what I can see. Look, they beckon, look at us, look at this world, look what's ahead, and just for a moment, I take my foot off the gas pedal.

The Burgeoning

THIS HAPPENED ONCE, and then it happened many more times; it is probably happening still. Probably it has happened, in a way, to someone you know. It happens to pretty girls, one of those pretty city girls. She was pretty, and young, nearly ripe, still whole, getting more whole, getting fuller. She was a sweet and lovely thing—that was the side of her we wanted to see, so that was the side of her we did see. Her mother loved her—and her Grandma loved her even more. It was amazing how lovable she was, but only to the women in her immediate family, who were her only apparent family. Men and beasts would love her also, but in different ways, in ways that made you reevaluate the ways in which we love. But her mother's love for her, and her Grandma's love for her, these were simple and straightforward pure loves. Her Grandma even made the pretty girl a very eye-catching red woven hooded capelet, which so suited the girl in all her burgeoning girlishness, that she wore it all the time, and became known as The Pretty Girl Who is Always Wearing That Red Hooded Capelet, though unsurprisingly, this moniker was soon distilled to just its most important elements.

One day, when she walked into the kitchen, her mother said, "Oh, there you are, my Pretty Girl. Please bring these to Grandma—there's a rumor that she's not feeling very well. Here, take her this freshly-baked soft, soft bread, and a bit of this sweet cream butter that she loves!"

And so The Pretty Girl did what she was told, and she took the basket, and set off for her Grandma's house, which was in the suburbs just outside the city, on the other side of a forest. In the middle of her walk through the forest, The Pretty Girl happened upon The Wolf. The Wolf was a Wolf, and had an innate wolfishness, which manifested itself in his longing to devour

The Pretty Girl, tear her apart and slurp her down whole. But there were others in the forest, actual men, real men, with real jobs, and who carried axes upon their broad hairless shoulders, and so The Wolf simply asked The Pretty Girl where she was headed. And The Pretty Girl, who did not yet know, had not yet learned not to engage, had not yet learned of any need to not always be her lovable, young, ripe self, said in her sweet and lovely way, "Oh, I'm going to my Grandma's house, I'm taking her this freshly-baked soft, soft bread, and a bit of this sweet cream butter that she loves!" And she held out her basket, as she said this, tilting it toward The Wolf, delicately lifting up the top, and, in a heedless rush of demonstration, or was it performance, lightly pushed her young white tender fingertips into the springy softness of the still-warm bread, which now exuded a fragrant steam.

"Oh?" he said. "Does she live very far from here?" The Wolf did not look long at The Pretty Girl's smooth tender fingertips fingering—kneading almost, nearly—the pulsating bread, wasn't it pulsating, like a living thing wrapped warm. He thought he might give himself away, surely by his dilating pupils if not by the protrusion growing with a pulse of its own, in his woollen trousers. He slid his paws behind his suspender straps and felt, for a moment, their tightening, the slight eager strain.

"Oh, I don't know," said The Pretty Girl. It was strange that she said this, because of course she *did* know exactly where her Grandma's house was, and therefore whether or not it was far away (it was rather far away, as are most of the things we set out for, rather far beyond our reach, no? In a most enticing way, a most thigh-clenching way). But she wanted to look longer at this wolfish face before her, his salivation, could it not be her salvation? His hunger, could it not be her hunger? How else was she to keep this moment, between two hungry creatures, facing off in a forest, that is on the one hand just a forest full of trees, but on the other hand, ten thousand other things? How many decades or centuries or millennia ago was it that a pretty girl first pretended to not know something for the sake of just several more moments with the most scrapingly, achingly, slice-to-ribbons set of sharpened teeth a pretty girl had ever been starved for?

The Wolf smiled at The Pretty Girl and waited.

"Oh, well. My Grandma's house is just on the other side of the forest. The first house. The suburbs." The Pretty Girl did not know what else to say. She swung her basket a little bit.

"That's fascinating," said The Wolf. He said it in a very sincere manner. "I am forever succumbing to novelty. New things, you know, things I have yet to touch. I have never seen a Grandma before, do you think I might see her too? Wolves don't have Grandmas, you know, and I would be so much obliged. Well? We can make a game of it, a date of it, I go one way, you go another, one of us will arrive first and wait for the other."

The Pretty Girl was still caught on the word, *date*, it was kind of a sweet-sounding word wasn't it, its sweetness not something she had noticed before. She blinked rapidly a few times, her breasts felt full and warm beneath her capelet. She was about to say something, but The Wolf had already nodded winningly, and wolfishly, at her, and started off on his way, assuming she would take the other. Which she did, feeling a feverish sort of blindness, a sensation as if she were the cool sweat coating a wide and long stream of fluttering silk ribbon, winding itself through the forest of its own accord, aiming for the house on the other side, aiming for the heart of The Wolf, who surely would arrive first, who would surely be waiting for her, heart exposed. She wound and wound herself through the trees, kneeling down on her knees occasionally to feel the thud of her knees on the dark forest soil, to feel the tearing of roots and stems as she yanked and ripped at bunches of wildflowers. She floated after a butterfly, she gathered nuts into her skirt, held some in her mouth. She stood still, and pictured him.

The Wolf was already there. He knocked at the Grandma's door. Knock. Knock. Knock. On your knees.

"Hello? My lovely, Pretty Girl, is that you?" the Grandma called.

"It's me," said The Wolf, his snarled lips near the seams of the door, nearly touching the wood, "And I've brought you some freshly-baked soft, soft bread, and a bit of this sweet cream butter that you love!"

"Oh I am all tucked into bed, do you mind just turning the outside knob counterclockwise, and the latch bolt will recede from the face plate, causing the bolt and the nut to shift, and the spindle to enter into the rose of the inside knob, and the push-button to unlock?"

The Wolf did as he was told, and the door opened wide. He launched himself over to the bed, fairly threw himself down on top of the Grandma, and ate her. He ate her so fast. He had not eaten in three days, and had just spent the last hour careening through the forest, salivating over The Pretty Girl's pungent unfurling. Best to devour this old one, tamp down on his lust for a moment, and be primed, steady, rock-solid for the one just about to be split open, sweet juice dripping, a ripe fig. He pressed the push-button on the inside knob, and locked the door. Then he settled himself in the Grandma's bed, which was still warm. She came.

Knock. Knock. Knock. *On your knees.*

"Hello? My lovely, Pretty Girl, is that you?" The Wolf pitched his voice. Almost to a scream.

The Pretty Girl shuddered at the sound of the voice. She did not feel like she knew it, but she rationalized: the rumor was that Grandma was not feeling very well, this was the reason for her visit, anyway, and so her voice was possibly gruff and hoarse from a sore throat, and so The Pretty Girl straightened her shoulders. Maybe she knew, somewhere, on some level of blood and hormones and fantasy, that it was The Wolf who had spoken to her from inside. But didn't she want The Wolf, wasn't that want pure and simple enough to darken all other thoughts and banish all misgivings?

"It's me," said The Pretty Girl, her mouth pressed full-on against the wood of the door as she spoke this, something hard against something soft. "And I've brought you some freshly-baked soft, soft bread, and a bit of this sweet cream butter that you love!"

The Wolf could barely lie still. He rustled under the sheets. "Just turn the outside knob counterclockwise, and the latch bolt will recede from the face plate, causing the bolt and the nut to shift, and the spindle to enter into the rose of the inside knob, and the push-button to unlock!" he shouted desperately.

The Pretty Girl did as she was told. She opened wide.

The Wolf pulled the covers up, he smoothed the covers back down, then up once more. "Just leave the freshly-baked soft, soft bread, and the bit of sweet cream butter that I love on the counter."

The Pretty Girl did as she was told.

"Come to bed," The Wolf commanded. There was a sliver of something glinting, on the very edge of his voice.

As if in a dream, or as if it was all she had dreamed of, The Pretty Girl took off her clothes. She climbed into the bed. She expressed shock at the sight of Grandma in that nightgown. It was so completely unbecoming, so very unfeminine. Would she become like that too, as an old woman? What became of old women? What became of pretty girls? She squirmed under the blanket. The Wolf edged closer to her. The Pretty Girl shivered now, moved restlessly against the sheets.

"Grandma, your arms are thick and flabby and hairy."

"The better to hug you with, my Pretty Girl."

"Grandma, your legs are very veiny and furry."

"The better to chase you with when we play games, my Pretty Girl."

"Grandma, your ears are so big and sharp."

"The better to hear your moans, my Pretty Girl."

At this, The Pretty Girl stopped writhing for a moment. But it was too late, she couldn't stop, the game was being played.

"Grandma, your eyes are so cold, so dark, so dangerous, how they gleam!"

"The better to see your near-perfect flesh, perspiring, blossoming, opening for me, my Pretty Girl."

The Pretty Girl stilled.

"Grandma, your teeth are like the teeth I have dreamed of, that would tear me apart, and give me my first breath."

"The better to devour you, your sweet and lovely naked body, to slurp you down whole."

The Wolf said these practiced words, and threw himself against The Pretty Girl. But she had opened her eyes as he said those words, she had opened her eyes as he fell upon her, and she had seen that they were old phrases, that they circumscribed all that she would ever see, through her Pretty Girl eyes. And in that moment, The Wolf just as quickly reeled forcefully back, found that he could not eat her, for she had grown old, in the playing of this game.

He shut his shining, black eyes. Back in the forest, he would find something exceedingly more delicate, more lovely, more simple. Something not just playing dumb. Something less formed.

Newfangled Creature

SHE IS FILLING IN as a pole fluffer again. The pay is bad. The street cred is okay-good. The story is pretty good. She is kind of into the poetry of it, even of the phrase itself, two nondescript words, nondescript but also seemingly contradictory—hard, soft. Good, bad. Mostly, it is because her friend Denise needs her to say yes, and so she says yes.

She met Denise years ago eating lunch at the place on the corner of Sunset and Echo Park Ave. They were fast friends. They both worked nearby. They both wore a lot of dresses in those days. It is funny to think about these days, versus those days—these being what you have, those being out of reach—especially on days when she is filling in as a pole fluffer. A lot of tasteful dresses in those days, where the fabric tightened over nothing, nothing was too tight or low or high. Denise was a little bit plump, but her dress would have been tastefully accommodating of her plumpness. Nothing squeezing anything. Tasteful dresses, where you couldn't see any evidence of underclothing, no bra straps sliding out of place, or lacy tips of anything, but you also couldn't see any evidence of *lack of* underclothing. Her own mother had been very clear on that point. None of those thin fabric skirts where your butt cheeks swung around like wobblecakes. Because if your butt cheeks were jiggling around, you were wearing a thong, or nothing at all, and then it was a slippery dippery slope from there, my child. And be sure nobody can see your bra, but that everybody can see that you're wearing a bra! Nobody wants to see your real breasts, no evidence of real breasts, my child! Cover it up, cover it all up, like white icing on a cake, make it smooth and sealed, all around. No peeking, no telling what kind of cake is under there. No telling if it's good, or bad.

It is not the most glamorous thing, pole fluffing, though when her supportive friends come to cheer her on in the smoky audience, they tell her she looks very good in her outfits. She does not know where Denise gets these outfits, but she is always ready with some new outfit. Denise calls her, frantic, someone is sick, or some misunderstanding about the schedule, can she please come in and do the show tonight, and she agrees, and next thing she knows she's looking up directions and driving to some new pop-up venue, and Denise is pulling her into some back door and shoving into her hands a shopping bag with a half-dress and maybe a couple of accessories. Usually, there is time to smoke a joint before digging into the shopping bag. A mask, or strands of beads, sometimes some shoes, a feathery hairpiece, a long cigarette holder, elbow-length gloves. There is a cloth bag, also, with a pile of silky-looking towels—the tools of the trade. They are surprisingly absorbant for looking so silky—must be some infomercial magic cloth. Whatever it is, it makes quick work of absorbing the oils and grease and sweat on the pole on the stage. Which is what she does, in between the burlesque pole dancing sequences. Wipe down the pole. In a sexy way, while wearing a flimsy lingerie evening gown with half the gown missing. Fluff the pole. Don't think about it. Just fluff it.

She turns her mind into a pole of fluff. The mind has taken the shape of a pole fluffer. Who knew what this was, what she was doing, with this pole, this fluff, a barbershop pole, hypnotic swirls, candy cane stripe fun. It never ends, eyes turn into the swirls, begin swirling in reflection, swirling in tandem. She can't see her reflection in anyone's eyes anymore, this usually marks some sort of psychotic break doesn't it?, break from others, their love, break from yourself, yourself away from yourself, yourself parting from yourself, outstretched fingertips slipping, can't quite reach. Hover in midair for one more moment. Notice the gap between fingertips. Far-gone. They will never, ever touch.

Fluff the pole. Don't think about it. Add a couple of pompoms, cheerleader pompoms, one at each end, one at the top, one at the bottom. Her twelfth-grade English teacher had also been the cheer coach. Mrs.

Summers. Cheercoach Summers. She had perfectly even white teeth and perfectly even blonde hair. There was a very straight part on the top of her neat yellow head. Sometimes she wore sweater sets, and sometimes she wore athletic-looking white T-shirts with the sleeves rolled up a little in a couple of very even folds. Her daughter was Lacey Summers, which everyone thought was great, because it sounded so porny, and Lacey had long straight hair, more of a dirty blonde, and whenever something moved out of place, which was rare, and they saw her bra strap, it was blindingly white. She had never seen such a bright white bra strap, in her life. Maybe it was just how it was pressed against her golden shoulder. So white, so clean. First snow.

Fluff the pole. Good or bad?

When she was thirteen, she was obsessed with the idea of being good. The summer after seventh grade, they took a family vacation to Marseille, and stayed in a hotel that consisted of six guest rooms. They had to go up the elevator in three trips, each ride up in the rickety little box could only carry one parent and one daughter and one large suitcase. A backpack could fit if it were sitting on top of the suitcase, but could not fit if it were strapped on one's back. The old man at the front desk gave her a large eight-by-ten photograph of himself, it was a glossy black and white publicity photograph, he was a magician in addition to owning the little hotel, and in the photograph he had a deck of playing cards fanned out in his left hand, and his right hand gestured in the air toward the cards like a shadow puppet, mysterious and a little bit menacing. Voilà, he inscribed onto the photo with a black marker. And then, Philippe, signed with a flourish, his marker ending in midair, his autographed name trailing off into space.

She was sitting with her family at a cafe when her goodness was tested. The table was very small, and round. There were four of them. The four of them were sitting around a round table, but somehow it felt like she was sitting facing her sister and mother and father, being interviewed, or interrogated. Beatrice had found a pack of cigarettes in a drawer of the desk in the hotel room, and had brought it out with her, and they were all trying to get her to smoke a cigarette. Not a whole one. Just try it. Come on. We're in a cafe in France. We have to all smoke a cigarette! She had refused. She thought back to the big banner. She had signed a big banner, just a big swath of yellow butcher paper really, that had been taped up on the outside of the auditorium at the end of Drug Abuse Resistance Education (D! A! R! E! DARE!). Just last May. She was never ever going to smoke a cigarette, ever, or do any drugs. Ever. Why would you do that. The special guest D.A.R.E. police officer had brought in a jar of black tar, that was the tar that sat in your lungs if you smoked. She couldn't believe she was sitting there, and her family wanted her to smoke a cigarette with them. What a circus. She sighed a little, as if they were children, and stared moodily over at the Frenchman at the next table over with his tousled hair and raggedy scarf. Save me, she thought.

At least the bakery next to the hotel had been mostly good. Except that one morning, when they got those croissants, and there were little yellow ants crawling around all over inside of the croissants.

When she was nineteen, she was obsessed with the idea of being good. She was in love with a guy, and he was in love with her, but he was a musician, and he had a musician girlfriend who was mentally unstable, and who was always on tour. Whenever she and the musician saw each other, they would exchange letters that they had written to each other when they were not together, when they were in their respective homes late at night, or while waiting in the car for something, or while at work. *I don't know*, she had written, *how long I should expect myself to survive off of being good. Solely off of* being good. Being good meant she and the guy could be best friends, being good meant bringing up his girlfriend in conversation all the time.

Talk about her, be good, talk about her as if she were in the next room. He was a philosopher-musician, the worst kind of person, nothing to hold on to, except words and sounds. His idea of being good was to stay with his girlfriend, because he loved her too, and because she was depressive and she needed him more. Whereas, she—well, she did not need him, because she was good and that meant not needing anyone or anything, especially not needing anyone with a girlfriend, except as a friend, except as a friend who demanded nothing.

Once, they did mushrooms in the park by his house, out in Valencia, where he lived because he lived with his brother, who was in school at Cal Arts, and while lying on the warm dry grass, she had realized she was in love, in love even with his cargo pants. But afterwards, when they were trip-recounting, she lied about it, to be good, and told a funny story about realizing she was in love with the playground, and wanting to marry the churning apparatus, and the wobbling wooden planked bridge, and the squeaky sun-cracked rubber swings, and she even made up something about how she had decided the playground's name was Jungle Jim, and how she had hallucinated that she and Jungle Jim would be married, and would slide down the slide together, in a drug-logic kind of way the playground was going to be able to slide down its own slide, with her, the blushing bride.

Denise's friend's friend, who is in town for some art show and who stops by the strip show, comes home with her after they all go to the diner, and crashes on the couch. She rambles on at length about pole fluffing. Although he was there, so how much more is there? Fluff it, swirl around it, fun fun fun. Magic-towel-sweat it, he deadpans. He gets it. They laugh and laugh and laugh.

In the morning, she tells him to come lie next to her in the bed. He clambers over onto the bed, nearly knocking over the plants on her side table. Watch out!, she laughs. Watch out for Count Draculus the Cactus!

And Jordan Cactuslano! Oh, he says, his hands hovering over her sleep-matted hair. Such a pretty flower. Such a pretty egg. Good egg. Hard, boiled, egg, she says. Shards, spoiled, egg, she says. Chimera between her legs, chimera of a body. Chimera of a head. Ladies and gentlemen, he says, standing up on the bed suddenly, in his underwear, let me present this newfangled creature...we call her...a woman! Voilà! She is half virgin, half whore. Half vamp-tramp-working girl, half innocent, proper housewife! They laugh and laugh and laugh. Sis boom bah! Break yourself, away from yourself!

She shuts her eyes. She does not part her eyelids. She thinks of writing a song, a spoof of a spoof, called The Detachable Vagina Song. Still shut. She tests them, for the gluiness of sleep. She keeps them shut. She doesn't move. She stills the morning. She stills the world. She wills him to still. The sheets beneath her, and him, are dark forest-green. The covers are askew. The window is on her right. The glass is not clear. Her ex-boyfriend had remarked upon this before, that her window was dirty. She windexed it, once for herself, twice for him. She couldn't clean the outside of the glass, how do I do that, she had asked him. Doublepane. He hadn't answered. Was it not important?

Such pretty flowers, he says again. She doesn't make a sound. She doesn't move. I would rather be beautiful than pretty, she says. Beautiful has something dirty, bloody, harmful about it. There is blood on your hands, with beauty.

Well, however it is, I like it.

Oh yeah? she says. You like my however-it-is flower?

She opens her thighs, beneath the heavy duvet. He closes them back together firmly, with a sense of finality, like he has just finished reading the last page of a very long book. She opens them again, clenches experimentally. Make the movements of squeezing when there is nothing, and soon, there might be wet, enough to make your mouth water. He gets up off the bed and goes back out to the couch, she hears him rustling, as if finding something in his pockets. He comes back and kneels on the bed, with a belt in his hands. She is surprised, he does not seem like the type of guy, this messy unkempt dude, to be walking around wearing a belt. But perhaps he *is* the type of guy to wear a belt for the sole purpose of being able to use it while having sex. She is startled, and pleased, that her brain has been able to come to this conclusion. She grins at him, her pussy suddenly gaining a heartbeat, she holds out her wrists.

In the mornings, she likes to have her back toward whomever it is, be facing a window, have the first things she sees be an empty field outside, a cold drifting fog.

R

When she was twenty-four, her father left her mother. It was kind of a late-in-the-game kind of thing, for sixty-year-olds to be separating themselves from their partners of almost forty years. She did not have forty of anything, had never done forty of anything. Forty ounces to freedom. Forty ounces was nothing. Weighed nothing. A bodiless light. Not so light as that, she could not see the light, any light, anywhere.

When she was twenty-four, her boyfriend of two years was bad. She herself was bad. There was something bad about her. Her boyfriend liked for her to sit on him, while he talked to other women on the phone. Sometimes he would lie on his stomach, propped up on his elbows, on the rug in the living room, and call his coworker Pam about something work-related, that would lead to just talking about random things, and she would step over him, and sit down on his butt, and give him a back massage. His hair was getting long then. She would try to get a sound out of him. She could take off all her clothes, she could pull his sweatpants off while he lay there, chatting away to Pam about her brother's upcoming visit, she could position her naked body and lay it right over his, her tits pressing into his warm bare back. He could squirm. She could stay put. He could wiggle and roll himself over so that he was lying on his back, and use one arm to wrestle her back into position on top of him.

In Bucharest, a young man had once taught her a game. He had claimed it was a game everyone knew, a party game, a European game it must have been. One person would lie on the ground, stomach down, eyes closed. And then someone else would have to lie down on top of the person on the ground, body on body, also stomach down. And then the first person, the person on the bottom, would have to try to guess the identity of the person lying on top of him or her. No sounds, no movements. If that first person guessed incorrectly, a third person would then lie down on top of the second person, and the second person would have to guess who the third person was. If the first person guessed correctly, the game would start over.

This sounded like a bad game. But she found herself wanting to play it all the time. Walking on the street, in Echo Park, in Eagle Rock, in the winter, in the summer, anytime, she thought about this game. She thought about it while she was lying on top of her boyfriend, but also while she was in line at the grocery store. Make a game out of nothing. Make rules and order out of air. Guess who is hurting you. Start over, do it again. Feel trapped.

In the afternoon, alone once more in the house after Denise's friend's friend has gone, she stands in front of her vanity, brushing her teeth. She looks at the old black-and-white photo of Philippe the magician-slash-hotel-owner. She wonders what he is up to. She should set him up with her dental hygienist whom she just discovered was a dental-hygienist-slash-comedian. She stares at the photo. Voilà. Voilà what? What was he showing? Empty space between his hands. This was it? Voilà-here-you-go-have-this-nothing? She says this out loud, and can suddenly detect the taste of gummy colas in her saliva, even through the mint of the toothpaste. She sniffs her snot in, hard. More sour saliva. She wishes she still lived in Little Tokyo, in that gigantic trapezoidal room in the loft with twelve-foot-tall windows where she could smoke a cigarette inside the house.

Voilà! A pop! of air in your eyes, forced open, not by anyone else, only by your own volition. Open. Popped open after the force of orgasm, under greasy forest-green sheets, legs scissoring like frogs under the covers. Popped! Open! After twenty-four minutes of meditation on dirty wood floorboards, white linen curtains billow, balloon. Pop, you will feel this puff of air in your eye, as part of your eye examination at the optometrist's office. See better, see more clearly, see more seeingly. Oh, I do, she nods at the vanity mirror, vigorously.

She wants to believe. Things are getting better, all the time. She looks down at Count Draculus the Cactus. She had named it to remind her of Bucharest. A frigid and gray city. Piles of layered rags masquerading as human, half-lifted out of manholes in the middle of the sidewalk, people descending into the urban earth for warmth. It was apocalyptic, neon billboards advertising something with half-naked women's bodies draped in parallel, identical, evening gown bathing suit combos. Denise would probably think those outfits perfect for pole fluffing. City full of wolfish dogs, eager, baring teeth, sad and sharp, slipping by. Once, the same night that young man taught her that strange party game, she got lost in an endless maze of Communist-era housing blocks. Two dogs slunk over in the snow. She felt suddenly drained, drunk, ice-cold, defenseless. Maybe the dogs here were so weak as to not pose any real harm? She had half-turned to look at one of them. She thought she saw, in the reflection of its eye, the possibility of one last burst of desperation, to survive, to make room for itself, to tear apart. She lightly cups her hand around the cactus now, testing the sharpness of its spines on her skin.

Somebody Else In The Room

The Very Beginning Part

LUCY AND JASON the Mason met in a poetry class at their neighborhood community arts center. Jason the Mason had been talking a lot in class, as per usual, words spilling for the sake of filling. Everyone already knew that he was an artist, stone work ("stoned work"), à la Andy Goldsworthy. It was the infamous class in which Jason claimed that it was not possible to feel more than one emotion at a time, and that often, in poetry, or otherwise, when someone was described as feeling two emotions at once, it was most likely, actually, one emotion *quickly followed* by another: rapid succession. At this, their teacher Brenda stood up. Brenda had been an actress in Los Angeles in the fifties, playing bit parts in *Beach Blanket Bingo* and a couple of the *Gidget* films, and then had moved to New York in the sixties to be a dancing showgirl at the Copacabana with her best girlfriend, and had been here since. You could still see the ghost of her glamorous past, in her long perfect white hair, straight, just a bit past her shoulders, curled in at the ends, a smooth moisturized forehead, and big, big glasses.

At Jason the Mason's grand claim, other people in the class had frowned in distaste, or general disagreement, but Brenda scraped her chair back. Metal on poured concrete. And what of Catullus, she said quietly. *Odi et amo?* Are you calling Catullus simple-minded? Are you arguing that what Catullus meant was, I hate, and then after I finish hating, I subsequently feel love?

Jason looked taken aback only for a second, and then grinned. Lucy gathered he was not used to people paying attention to anything he said, to people taking him seriously. In the first session of class, he had told her, outside, during their bathroom break, that he didn't think poetry should be about feelings. Lucy hadn't even been sure quite what to make of that, had been chewing for way too long on a small misshapen hardened Clif bar, and merely said Huh, because she had suspected he was just looking for an argument, and she had had better things to do. He was too pale. His hair was too perfectly coiffed. His pants looked like they had been ironed. She hadn't said she had better things to do, but she was pretty good at arranging mostly the muscles around her eyes into an expression which said this same thing.

The Beginning Part

After class one day, they had stood at opposite ends of the quad smoking, but had both converged at the trash can to throw out their butts at the same time. She knew this was coming. It had taken steps forward to get to the trash can, steps during which they both could see what was coming. What do you think about crushes? he had asked her. Oh man, she'd said. I could talk about that forever. He raised an eyebrow. Yeah? he said. We're just going to get right into it, huh? She laughed and asked, what else is there to talk about? Sports? In fact, she was starved for conversation about love and hate and crushes. She'd had a surprising trail, in the past few years, of disastrous affairs with several French and French-American guys, in France, in L.A., and even here in New York. Stereotype-defying French guys who avoided all talk of love, even though she'd thought she made it clear she was interested only in talking about theoretical or past loves, not love in the present tense. In fact, the more she fought against the idea of love for herself, the more she felt compelled to talk about it from a distance, in the most general terms. Jason the Mason grinned, and invited her over for a drink.

She showed up, he grabbed two beers, they sat on the couch. It got really out of hand. Out of their hands. She had no hand in it. She never even took any of her clothes off, she was wearing a woolly dress and woolly tights. He put his hand down her tights, but barely, under her underwear, but barely, never even let his fingers puncture inside. She was so wet. So swollen. A water balloon down there, a real juicy one. A couple times, she started to push her own hand down her tights, down her underwear, but she would just barely get to her pubic hair, barely brush it, and she would have to remove her hand, it was just too much. The slipperiness was not to be touched. It felt out of control. At each other's throats. And then they would back away, look at each other, almost in shock. Breathing hard, panting. Audible sounds of swallowing. Fuck, he gritted out. Frustrated. Goddddddamnit, he texted her, afterwards.

The Middle Part

In the fall, one night, after burgers, they had strolled around a little bit in the park, it was getting colder then, he led them to sit down on the side of a monument with a flag pole, tomb of unknowns, and piles of carnations left over from the Veteran's Day wreath-laying ceremony. All is fair in love and war basically means that nothing is fair in love and war. It was only about ten or twenty minutes spent there, huddled in the cold, half-hidden in the darkness by the flowers and trees and bushes, they talked about holiday plans while he absently played with her hair. He leaned in and bit her ear, a bright and startling thing.

She told him the sad news about how the tree outside her bedroom window had lost all its leaves. She told him the sad news about how she couldn't find her corduroy pants.

That's what you get for taking your pants off all the time in front of strangers.

I don't do that!, she said, laughing. She continued leisurely rambling out small words into the cold air, talking about hoping to find them once she unpacked her winter things.

But you wore them during the summer, right, so...

I don't wear pants at all during the summer!

Didn't you? I remember you wearing them.

Um, no way. I would never wear corduroys in the summer. I think I would know.

Really? I remember you wearing them, he said, laughing. Because I remember putting my hands in them.

She laughed too, surprised, pleased, warmed, everything was open and easy and free that night. Oh really, she said.

Yeah, I do.

Well, maybe you put your hands in them last winter. Anyway, they're pretty tight, you probably couldn't even get your hands in there.

Oh, I think I could probably manage to do it.

The End Part

I need to turn over a new leaf, new me, Lucy said to Jason. They were sitting up side by side in the strange-sized bed. She had thought it was a queen, but it turned out to be only full, and now, it seemed to be somewhere middling, between twin and full. They had been swallowing up secrets and sticklike difficult words for three months now. Three rounds down to zero. Three rounds up to trouble.

Oh? Jason said, but it wasn't a prompting-type of Oh. It sounded like a question, but ended with a period. He was closer to the window, and was looking out the window. There was a whole backside of apartment buildings, the ones that lined the south side of 8th Street, separated by two rows of backyards—like perfectly white lined up teeth—from the row of apartment buildings which lined the north side of 9th Street. All up and down these numbered streets, it was the same.

It was cold this winter, and with no curtains or blinds, Lucy could feel the cold emanating from the window. There must be cracks, well, she could see one crack along the windowsill for sure, and, or, maybe it was just the glass. The panes had been replaced by thin sheets of pure ice. Perhaps it was Jason who had replaced them. While she was sleeping, while he was unable to sleep. Lucy squinted hard at Jason, but his head was still turned, and she supposed this meant he had not felt the force of her squeezing lids. He wasn't saying a thing.

At some point, she could no longer tell what they were doing in her bed, she and Jason the Mason. Jason, the last guy she had sex with. Where they were going. They were trying to do something, in this bed, trying to get somewhere, get at something. But where? Where can you get? And on a bed, no less? How did they end up here, on an elevated platform of cushions, who was supposed to be worshipping at this altar, what were they doing that deserved being done on a dais?

There was nothing sacred, that she could fathom. Fathoms below, fathoms below. But even below, there wasn't anything, as far as she could tell. And at that point, she thought she could tell pretty far. There would be nothing to unearth: fine, dry, tasteless dirt, tasteless earth.

Then they were wrapped around each other as tightly as possible. She couldn't see him, but the room was dim anyway, but maybe her eyes were closed. He pushed himself into her, again and again, and her fingers were slipping on sweat, and at some point she could just tell. She could just tell him, I thought that we were going to turn into each other, one into the other, we were going to Freaky Friday it, and finally, she would get to be someone else.

Forever, people ask her, What are you? Many people in the world get asked this question, but there are also many people in this world, who do not get asked this question.

If enough men press their penises into her vagina, maybe she can turn into someone who does not get asked this question.

What are you?

A poet.

No, no. *What* are you? Like...

Oh. I'm American.

No, you know what I mean. Where are you from?

California.

No, like, *what* are you? Like, Korean, Japanese, Chinese...

Are those my only options?

Why don't you ask her something else? Ask her *who* she is. Hunger for a different kind of knowledge. Challenge her. Don't make her play dumb. With the first guy she had sex with, she didn't have the articulate thought, the death wish, to return someone else. She thought—assumed—she would come out the other side the same person. She thought she had some things going. She was out of school, but not so naïve—it was her third year at a horrifying editing job surrounded by termites and ghosts. This was in 2004, and that fall, all of her coworkers came forward as staunch Republicans. One of her coworkers started blasting conservative talk radio. Another one was constantly forwarding her emails about Warring Against Terror. She didn't come forward, she was a secret.

She was warring against an uncapitalized terror, also known as her relationship with her first boyfriend. They lived in a large, old, shady one-bedroom place, on North Clark Drive, in West Hollywood, though how exactly the two of them ended up there is beyond her at this point, and at that point, well, she wasn't in the business of analysis. She never had been. Less bridges crossing back and forth across her corpus callosum. No cause and effect. No meaningful patterns. No derived significance. She had eyed a place in Echo Park, and he had finally agreed to drive out to see it, and then had nixed it—too dangerous. It had pretty yellow stucco, and an open courtyard.

She slept on the couch sometimes, those years in West Hollywood, as demonstration of how much she hated him. She slept in the car once or twice, to demonstrate the same thing, though she believes this, even for her, was on the brink of extreme. One street over was Robertson Drive, another two blocks was the Beverly Center, and sometimes she took pleasure in dressing as sloppily as possible, shapeless gray sweatpants, strange boots, an old hoodie, and going out late at night around the empty high-end retail streets, traipsing along Robertson, or San Vicente, sometimes she went to the Beverly Center, when the shops had closed but the mall was kept open, because there was a movie theatre on the top floor, atrium level, and sometimes she would go see a movie, but often she would just wander around the silent levels of the mall, sit momentarily in the lounging areas that during the daytime on weekends were occupied by weary men waiting on their ladies.

In West Hollywood, they were also two blocks away from the Cedars-Sinai Medical Center, which turned out to be quite convenient, because she ended up having to go to a gynecologist a bunch that year, yeast infection, urinary tract infection, vaginal random infection. Her boyfriend felt very down every time she couldn't have sex with him, even though it was the sex they were having that was making it painful to pee, or making her feel like she constantly had to pee, or fucking up her flora, forcing her to down probiotics to neutralize her fauna.

The Figuring Out What Type of Girl She Is Part

As a girl, as a certain type of girl, maybe, you get used to guys saying Next time we'll split one burger, or Hopefully someday I'll get to try out your mom's cooking, or When we go eat there I'll tell you..., and feeling pleasure at this existence of a future, when you will continue to do things together, and then quickly reminding yourself not to feel this pleasure, reminding yourself it means nothing, don't take it seriously, literally. Because, as this certain type of girl, you are consistently dealing with this type of guy, who turns into a ghost, and what can you do, because you have never prioritized niceness in a guy over everything, or indeed, anything, else.

The Naked Ghost Man Part

There is a naked ghost man in her room. Sometimes he wanders, barefoot, into the rest of the house. The kitchen is small, so it doesn't take him long to walk through it. There is a long hallway, between the bedroom and the kitchen, though—that takes a while. The intricate parquet floors are glossy, but also prone to splinters, especially along the sides closer to the walls. She doesn't worry about the naked ghost man, he treads softly, each step a quick light pat.

Sometimes the naked ghost man reads in the living room, but he only ever sits in the right corner of the couch. Sometimes he fries up a couple of eggs for breakfast, eaten with toast cut diagonally, and salsa. When she's run out of salsa, he'll use marinara sauce from some old jar in the back of the refrigerator.

Last night she came home from work, late, midnight, and the naked ghost man was sitting at the piano by the front window. He had his hands hovering over the keys, fingertips barely on the keys, his head slightly bent down and forward. She can't ever really see him, the naked ghost man. The house is pretty shadowy, and she always misses it, the moment in which she might be able to see his face. Sometimes, she is close, she thinks. She sees it, peripherally, or senses the full-on frontal look, but when she turns, gone. She thinks she turns slowly, to give him a chance to turn away.

She didn't have to work today, so she made herself a ham and swiss and tomato sandwich, and sat down on the couch to watch the movie *Lust, Caution*. The naked ghost man gets up from the piano bench and sits down on the couch next to her, in his usual corner. The version of the movie she finds in a dusty case on the shelf doesn't have the English subtitles. She can't understand enough of the Mandarin—and it switches to Shanghainese and Cantonese, which makes it even more impossible. She does understand, when in the scene on the double-decker bus that one night, the guy moves up front to sit by the girl and says thank you, and she says why, and they both smile, but more to themselves, since they can't see each other—they are both facing forward on the bus, and after thanking her, he has moved back to two rows behind her. She understands that the girl's not asking why. Her why ends with a period. She understands that much.

She doesn't look as much, when she passes the Smith and 9th stop these days. She still listens to the announcement droning out the name. Smith and 9th Street. But it is smaller now, and shrinking still, a watery puddle evaporating to coin-sized, then a pinpoint. Not yet, but she can see it. If she doesn't have to move too much, make too much of an effort, if she's not distracted by a book she's reading or her phone, she still looks out onto the platform. But only if she doesn't have to twist around in her seat, or lean her head over way to one side. She still looks. Each person who glides by, who is not Jason the Mason, makes the sound of a thunk, a blip cutting up the panorama. Person, not him, empty space, person, not him, empty space, empty space, person, not him, empty space.

Oh, he sees me, she had thought. Someone finally sees her. Before Jason the Mason, she had only ever experienced sight as emanating from undesirable French dudes whose soul-probing pupils seemed intent upon turning her into a swollen wedge of triple crème Saint-André cheese.

On the Fourth of July, the last time she saw him, he had mentioned something about something being because she was a ghost. I'm not a ghost, she had said, laughing, because it was her habit to disagree with everything, and to laugh when confronted with something confusing.

Now, she doesn't see him, nor is she seen any longer. Now, there is just this naked ghost man, drinking a beer at her kitchen table, or sitting on the couch next to her watching a movie.

The Sorry Part

He apologized to her, in a text message. She knows she is not supposed to count this, because this is a text message, and also, because he has not said anything to her in eight months, during which he has moved to California, met some girl on a bus, and married her. But, but, that was what he was apologizing for.

She can't help it. She nods when Caroline says these supportive friend things, or, probably, they are not even supportive friend things, they are, like, decent human behavior reminders. She nods, but inside, she is very happy. This is a big deal, inside of her, away from Caroline, and conventional world decency. This is a big deal, because he exists again. This is a big deal, because it's him they are talking about, and Caroline doesn't know him. She admits that she herself doesn't even really know him, know *know* him, because how can they, she, anyone, et cetera. BUT. She certainly knows him more than Caroline knows him. And, she has certainly known more men, loved and hated and felt ambivalence, toward more men, in her life, than Caroline has.

Caroline was someone Lucy had really wanted to befriend, right when she met her. You could tell she had been a bold child. Lucy had not been a bold child. She had not wanted to be, had not known to want that until much later. As a child, she had been pink, faint, a smudge. She had been like the person, or thing, you saw before you put on your glasses.

The 38th Street Diner, situated as it is, in the middle of the block, on the south side of the street, is in perpetual shadow. It will never see the light of day, or at least not until or unless a majority of the surrounding high-rises disappear. The important thing about this is that she will never be able to sit in a window booth at the 38th Street Diner and be bathed in sunshine. She will never spend the morning of a 4th of July, with a guy in a green T-shirt and ironed pants, with whom she is in love, who broke her heart, later that day, about whom she would later think, I can't believe this is the guy that has wreaked this, streaked such unavoidable red tape over so many future years, some guy, some pale average looking guy, in ironed pants, with whom she once had that 4th of July breakfast in that one diner in the sunlight when her heart felt as clean and bright and alive as the sun pouring in through the glass.

Caroline picks at her cuticles, and then resumes saying words like "not cool" and "happy" and "but" and "else," and so Lucy tunes out again. It is a very specific mode she has, and she thinks maybe everyone has it, when they talk to their mothers on the phone, basically a tuning-out, but she thinks some people might not have it as much, because then wouldn't they recognize it when someone was tuning them out and stop talking on and on? Or maybe not? In any case, Lucy thinks she has it more, maybe because she is a water sign, and prone to watery zoning out, and escapism at all times.

She thinks about how many people she has in her life, who basically say the things her mother would say, who basically say what she expects them to say, and then what use? Why say it, why meet up to listen to it? Not even actually listen to it, just sit across from it in a diner booth while tuning it out?

The Very End Part

Sunday morning she called out sick from work. The naked ghost man was nowhere to be found. A ghost of a ghost—how was this even possible? She sat on her bed, legs undercover, cold light leaked leaflessly through the cold window glass pane. She went on Facebook and looked up Jason the Mason. She selected him from a short list of Jasons. She sat across from his photo, a photo in which he smiled head-on, straight-on, unblinkingly, smiling his usual mouth-closed smile, his usual smile, which looked like a U, like the mouth on a smiley face. He was sitting at a wooden picnic table, it looked like the back patio of some bar in Oakland or Berkeley or San Francisco, holding a pint of beer, typical.

What was special about this photo was that it had been posted by his new wife whom he had just met on a bus five months prior, who probably took it, who probably was sitting straight across the table from him, who was probably the person he was looking at, head-on, and smiling at, that usual U-shaped smiley face smile.

And this special photo, she had posted on his page, and posted it with a heart, and underneath, were a couple likes, and a handful of comments from his mother and sister who were always commenting, and from his wife, who was always responding to comments by his mother and sister and sometimes his father too, and a few comments here and there from his friends, some of whom were like EW OH U GUYS, aka stop being so sick and so corny, how do you live like this, how can you live like that? was what she was thinking, sitting by herself on her bed on a cold February morning, instead of making money at her job, at one of her two part-time jobs, and she was thinking:

I suppose it's best that we ended, I could never stand his looks, the way he looked at me.

I suppose two corny people found each other.

There is nobody else in the room with me.

There is nobody else taking a photo of me.

I am smiling, in a beautiful, open-mouthed way, at nobody. And then re-worded:

I am not smiling, in a beautiful, open-mouthed way, at anybody.

Loose Morals

DO YOU THINK that's funny? the Detective's mouth was very close to her ear, and instead of shouting, he seemed to be stroking the words along his vocal cords, his throat, coaxing them along, like a hand caressing gravel.

No, the Hussy sobbed. She splayed her hands on the smooth hardness of the concrete wall. And yet she *had* been laughing, but didn't the man know that laughing and hurting stood back to back, laughter and tragedy, laughter and guilt, menace, blood?

Loose morals, they had chorused. Loose morals, the Detective muttered into her ear now. She stifled a hysterical sound. She twitched her hips back and forth, stomped her feet. It was Amendment #1362 that she had broken. Loose morals, Amendment #1362. Commoners called it the Carpet-Drapes Anomaly; the more rotten, post-millennial crowd referred to it as the Streets-Versus-Sheets Anomaly. Question number one: does your sexual behavior match your public persona, your most ostensible self? Question number two: if they set the Detective loose on you, will you behave? Question number three: can they find a way, a reason to lock you up?

She had been caught strolling up and down Robertson Boulevard, just one block west of the old Beverly Center mall, in sweatpants and a ratty T-shirt that read UCLA Bruins Athletics Department 1994. The surveillance cameras had shown her to be guilty of a mismatch: that space—the gap, the slit, the pussyhole catcunt—had on numerous past occasions—*recorded* occasions—proven culpable, capable of being both slice-knife sharp (intercourse that drew bloody scratches), *and also* muffled-soft engulfing (intercourse like the wet, matted-fur undulations of mammalian beasts). Not only did the Hussy's sweatpants and shower slippers belie her sexual nature, but she seemed horrifically—*illegally*—mutable within her sexual deviancy.

The Hussy pressed her hot cheek against the concrete so that she could stare the Detective full in the face. His eyes narrowed at her, he was thinking things about her, he must have been running an old TI-82 brain, which was not compatible with the ability to hold two seemingly contradictory truths at one time. The Resistance group had a perpetual huddle of techno-engineer nerds who worked on research and construction of brain upgrades, though there were inevitable failures of technology to capture and/or analyze the subtleties of morals, loose or firm. There was the tragedy of the Resistance Leader's Daughter, for instance, who had assassinated the former Police Chief, and then been accidentally taken out by one of the updated Resisters who had read—incorrectly—her flirtations while she was still undercover. An old, natural brain would never have made such an error.

She squirmed, and drawing her knee up as tightly and forcefully against the wall as she could, she let snap suddenly the heel of her foot backwards and up, into the groin of the Detective. He let out a small oof, a soft small boy sound, and then stumbled back slightly into the shadows of the overhang; in such shadows, his own five-o'clock shadow looked especially sinister.

The Detective recovered himself and returned to her, the hard fabric planes of his uniform once again abrading her back. He trained his chameleon eye on her. It was one of the New World Order government's first mandates for law enforcement Detectives to be staffed by officers with implanted chameleon eyes. This must be a joke, the citizenship incanted. It was not enough of a joke. They said people with chameleon eyes would be able to see everything. Nothing would escape notice. Surveillance at all angles.

The Detective rummaged around behind the Hussy's back. She rubbed her cheek against the concrete wall, hoping for the sting of breaking skin to bring something sharp into focus. He brought out the law book. Time for a read-aloud.

He paged through the book, paper sounds, thumbing sounds, and began intoning.

Mumbojumbomumbojumbo, he muttered against her ear. Amendment #1362, he jabbered. Loose morals, they chorused.

The old law books were written in the language of the New World Order's previous incarnation, the Old World Order. That language had been extinct from everyday usage for six hundred years.

She listened to the wash of mumbojumbo, and was led away. He propelled her down the cement hallway, through a pile of ramps and passages and narrow corridors that intersected at haphazard crossings, as if laid down in the shape of pick-up sticks mid-game.

§

ZOOMPP ZOOMPP, the wall thudded. Question number four: how much time had passed? The Hussy squirmed around in the small cot in the cell, and turned toward the noise. The small opening between her cell and the next cell was reverberating with the thudding. She peered up and through the hole in the wall and came face to face with a woman in a red hooded cape.

Red Widow, she said by way of introduction. Hussy, the Hussy said. The Red Widow nodded. Yoohoo, Hussy said, Amendment #1362? The Red Widow nodded, and then lifted the red hood away and back from her head. Her hair was coiffed in perfect red waves.

More specifically, we're here for Sounds, the Red Widow informed her. Do you feel a beating pitter-pattering there between your legs, she asked her. The Hussy said nothing. Then she nodded. The other woman's face, now no longer shadowed by the overhang of the hood, looked remarkably like her own face. Or, at least, like how her face looked the last time she had checked. Since that last time, she had been doled out punishment cuts to the cheeks, and her face was very likely no longer the same.

We're here for Sounds, the Red Widow said again. And then the Hussy understood. The women in this wing, all of them, had been booked for the same specific violation of Amendment #1362—for a Sensation #4 Mismatch: Sounds/Hearing. Her sexual sounds had not matched her sweatpants.

The Hussy realized her hands had curled and bunched into fists. She and the Red Widow stared at each other through the opening. The Hussy began laughing, and the Red Widow joined in. Others down the entire corridor of cells also began to laugh. Then, the Hussy screamed. She screamed for blood. As blood. As sharp, wet beast. And down the corridor, the others began screaming too; the sounds pulsated, louder and louder.

Year Of Righteousness, Year Of Confetti

IN THE CAR on the way home from LAX, my father is driving and he and my mother are talking about how when the two of them go to the airport to catch a flight these days, these years, they have to call a cab. "It's very expensive, twenty bucks, so forty bucks there and back," my mother says. I ask calmly, "You can't ask a coworker to take you?"

"It's a hassle," she says.

Why is there nobody, is all I can think. I ask, "Well, has anything new opened in Irvine?" And so we talk instead about the arrival of new restaurants, new branches of large corporations, new buildings.

In the guest bedroom where I am staying are hung framed paintings and illustrations I did in high school, that can pass as somewhat decent. I unzip my luggage and pluck out the bag of toiletries, leaving undisturbed the rest of the huge lump of clothing I'd forcefully compacted into the bottom half of the suitcase. I lie down in the bed. There are many decisions we make that lead to there being nobody.

In the morning, I am reminded by the light beaming in through the blinds that this is indeed Orange County, California, and I have indeed moved back in with my parents, and this is my life. In my bitterness, I grimace at the window and accuse the sunlight of feeling clean and suburban.

The next week, it's cold. June gloom. My feet are freezing and by noon, I'm still in my pajamas, unshowered, listening to my European playlists. I wouldn't mind a cocoon for a room, boiled wool walls, white sheets, smoothly curved vertices. I would feel better about languishing if it were appropriately hot here. It's not appropriately hot. It's very cold. There's a lot of construction that happens, and construction-related sounds. Although the homeowner's association ensures that it only happens during restricted hours, Mondays through Saturdays 8–6, none on Sundays.

I think about Budapest, Croatia, Romania, Berlin, Turkey, the bug in the soup I had in Sofia. I think about Morocco, and about getting *konnichiwa* yelled at me more times than I could have ever imagined, and I thought I could imagine a lot. I think about circling the Colosseum slowly, completing only about a third of an arc around its circumference, in the pouring rain. I think about other things I have done in the pouring rain: leaned over the railing along the river in Prague, walked home through the hilly sidewalks of Westwood from the UCLA campus, made out with a guy on a rock at a beach somewhere along the central coast of California. I imagine that in the pouring rain, my eyes look shiny, a stone fountain maiden blinded by water. I imagine that in the pouring rain, I disintegrate more slowly than usual, that maybe we all do.

Stuck at my parents' house, I try to recreate a very particular atmosphere, playing French electropop, in the tiny guest bedroom with its glass-topped desk and a cushioned swivel office chair digging itself into four tiny graves in the beige carpet. The music doesn't sound right, against this glass desk, against the cracks of light coming in through the white window blinds, it doesn't sound right with construction roaring monotonously.

$$\text{\textit{R}}$$

I get a part-time job in retail, at an expensive women's apparel and home accessories store. I have to look nice and put-together there, and emanate warmth and encouragement in the dressing room. I get to be the opposite of myself there.

"So what's your story? Are you in college? Taking some time off from school? What're you up to?" another new girl asks during training. Someone named Hailey or Heidi or Holly is giving us an overview of the company's general history and philosophy, but I am really only looking forward to the part on protocol to follow if we suspect we see a shoplifter—there are code words involved.

"Oh, no, no," I laugh good-naturedly, from deep within my retail customer service Bright Mode. "Done with college long ago," I say, but I hope not in a mean, condescending way, not an oh-I'm-so-far-advanced-beyond-college-and-you kind of way, because that's not at all what I mean. What I mean is, are you fucking kidding me, I'm Chinese and from Irvine, which means I graduated from a respectable four-year university when I was twenty-one, no questions asked.

While we are sitting there, in our training circle, one of the managers tells us she did voices for toys when she was younger. Everybody nods gamely. I am the only one who speaks up to ask, "Um, what does that mean, voices for toys?"

At my job in that store, dressed in narwhal-print silk blouses and palazzo pants and spouting all sorts of nonsense to women in the dressing room, I am suddenly outspoken. I will say anything to circumscribe this new opposite self into place.

It keeps me busy, being there.

The week before leaving for Europe was full of frantic packing. One night, I met up with Sam for drinks. The circumstances felt abnormal. To have known each other from work, and now, suddenly, we had to exchange phone numbers, and now, suddenly, I was straightening up my kitchen, my coffee table, and now, suddenly, he was calling because he was lost, and look, I was answering my phone for once, fascinated that this small event had officially started, and I slid my feet into my flip-flops, ran out the front door, out the front garden, into the bright May dusk, the asphalt hill of my lovely palm-tree-lined street empty as usual, downtown high-rises stretching smoggily over behind the hill, and I took leaping giant steps in my miniskirt, in the middle of the street, around the curve.

This was what it was like, when you had quit your job, when you hadn't started your new one yet, which was part-time anyway and in another country, and you had nothing you had to do but meet up with Sam and walk down the hill from your house to Sunset Boulevard and drink $2.50 margaritas that would surely give you headaches that unfurled like giant night-blooming flowers.

&

My cousin Lana came to visit me in Marseille during her winter break, and we decided to go to Paris for New Year's. It turned out Sam was going to be in Paris at the same time, to interview someone for his dissertation. I tried to explain to Lana who this friend was. "A work acquaintance from home, from L.A. Well, a friend. But you don't know him. Actually, I don't know him that well, I've technically hung out with him once, and that one time, I slept with him."

Lana and I were staying with Alex, my supervisor's son who lived in Paris. He had a sort of intense, smoldering stare that I felt like I had seen more on Frenchmen than elsewhere, but it's possible I am just myth-building. Most of this staring was directed at Lana. She had no idea. The first chance we got to ourselves, I asked her what she thought of him. "I think he likes you," I said. Nobody made much of this, but I knew it. I had seen his gaze, hovering mid-air, meeting nothing, falling short, emanating from one side only, lots of times. It made me slightly sick, slightly sympathetic. I didn't say anything else. But I didn't have to, the way the weekend continued. I felt vindicated, more and more. In life, I was often wrong, but the more time passed, the more I was sure I was right about this one thing.

For New Year's Eve festivities, Alex invited us to his friends' house party, and I invited Sam. Not too long into the evening, it was visible even to the naked eye of any drunken innocent bystander, how hard Alex was trying to hit on Lana, and how uninterested she was. For much of the night, I sat slouched in the crummy depths of a red couch next to three girls playing a Wii game that involved cooking, using the Wii gadget like a beater, or like a frying pan handle, or cracking open eggs. I was eating imitation crab sticks which were all the rage in France—they ate them like potato chips. Or rather, I ate them like potato chips: plain. They ate them like crudités: with a white sauce dip. Sam came over and sat down, not bothering to gesture for me to give him room, just wedging himself into the narrow space between me and the armrest at one end. He held out his hand. I looked down, clearly, clear-eyed, feeling not quite cold-sober, but seeing the hand, and seeing myself see the hand. I placed my hand, open, to meet his, just for a moment.

I looked around warily, expecting to see Alex hitting on Lana in some lurid corner. At the same time, I had to deal with other things. I couldn't fucking blow that balloon. I was allergic to the unseen cat. I couldn't stop eating those surimi sticks, even though they were covered in confetti I had to pick off before I could eat them. I really wanted to start smoking cigarettes, and there was no one to stop me.

Sam stuck his head into the space between my shoulder and neck, his long moppy curls feeling cool, and he leaned in closer, sticking his hand out again. I couldn't see his face. Or, I made sure not to look at his face. I stood up, headed out to the balcony.

A week after my re-entry into the U.S., my mother and father and I pick up my grandparents and take them to lunch in Hacienda Heights. I help my grandma in and out of the car, and I help her buckle her seatbelt. Afterwards, my father asks me if my grandparents seem to have aged a lot this time, after seeing them for the first time in a year. "Yes," I say, and don't say anything else, even though he leaves room there to say something else. But I don't. I don't know what to say. The room that is there has never before been big enough for me to jump into, leap into its depths, and it doesn't change now. When the time has passed, he just nods, too. Actually it is more he and my mother who feel older to me, their bodies fragile, small as if I am seeing them from far away.

People move or travel abroad and then return home a new person, transformed—this happens all the time. The first shower I took in my parents' house was a revelation. The water pouring out of the showerhead was insanely pleasurable, extraordinarily abundant. I could barely handle it, the unwavering heat and force and density of all of this water, rushing at me. But after three days, I no longer noticed it at all.

&

I could feel it, I could see it, the dotted-line diagram, the indicator arrows, showing me desire and directional flow. I was standing outside on the balcony, it was the New Year, it was 1 a.m. and it was motherfucking cold, but I would have rather been in the motherfucking cold than been back inside inhaling the cat dander allergens that had been kicked up from all the hard-partying Frenchmen with their confetti-blowers and noisemakers. Sam pulled open the sliding glass door, I heard it rolling like so much machinery coming to life, he stepped out, his black coat's collar cutting black wool angles on either side of his cheekbones. He had a cigarette wobbling between his lips, and his eyes hit mine for an instant, before he turned to push the door shut, and then stepped over to the far end of the balcony. Something rustled way down below us, near the train tracks. Where he was standing, in the corner, there was no glass, only the wall after the glass of the sliding doors had ended.

In one moment, a million synapses were firing in my brain of brains, mind of minds, not the heart, the threat of hearts. On that balcony, we spoke like this, fifteen feet apart, in the coldness, the darkness, the newness of the new year, about what, about things I was always desperate to speak about, especially in the cold, the dark. About the newness of life, about living near train tracks, about people and travel and what they do and what it does. But then, finally, I was too cold, and things were swerving, the universe, its intentions, its will—it was incredibly strong, wasn't it? And I would never be able to resolve or reconcile pieces then or later, but when I had made the tiniest degree of a movement toward a decision, when I was headed inside, Sam was calling me over, to the corner, where nobody would be able to see us, and I might have just disappeared and left friends and obligations and righteousness behind in a flailing, falling pile, which, if you just worked your hand into the bottom, and flicked your wrist, the pieces would fly up, weightlessly, and would take such a sweet time to float gently back to the earth.

In a way, it seemed like I didn't actually have to do any thinking, or move even the tiniest degree. Sometime in the last few years or so of my life, a change had been made, a decision was formed and dispatched, and it was in my blood, you see, and I laughed, loud, free, and shook my head, no, no, leaving Sam to understand, to turn his head back down to look at the tracks below, and finish his cigarette in the sharp, black cold.

Back inside, both on the couch, his eyelashes looked like stars, as if wet. I had thought, before seeing him in Paris, about the wild mess of hair he'd had that night in May in L.A., when we were swimmy with margaritas, but it had been cut, and it only charmed me more, that it was cut shorter on the sides and in the back, and left longer in the middle, the longest portion falling forward in waves into his eyes. It looked cocky. It made me laugh.

I'm not sure which one of us was thinking this, because we both turned to each other and laughed, in the same way that made me think—realize even—that either one of us could have been thinking of the same thing, or if not of the same thing, the same sentiment, and what did it matter what the thing was if it made you feel the same way?

"I think that's important," I heard myself saying, "laughing about the same things."

"How do you know we were laughing about the same thing?" he asked teasingly, and I was struck by the fact that he was able to say this teasingly, and how this validated me, and how sometimes you are right, but that doesn't save the day, much less your world. I pushed him. I had learned this from someone three someones ago, pushing, pushing to get what you want, even if it meant pushing yourself into the moist brown soil in hopes of hiding and growing something at the same time.

&

When I think about Sam now, I think about the fluttering energy of skin and skinniness, the fervid bright, the feverish insomnia, the constant stream of charge and compulsion. I think about the squawking inhalation of his laughter, like raucous dragging gasps, grasps at air. The steady hum of isolation and being by yourself, an only child. The wandering, fumbling, the mistakes, the blundering, the rashness. I think about how he called me sweetheart, and how I allowed myself to like it.

"You don't have to isolate yourself so much, you know," he had said that night of margaritas and sex. I probably said whatever. I probably rolled my eyes. But what he said had turned me transparent, for a moment. For a moment I didn't have to say anything, and he could see me. I wanted to disappear into the couch cushions, but he was sucking on my lips. I said, "Yeah, so you know me, so then what?" I said it in a way that indicated I did not care either way. I couldn't be bothered. I could only be seen for a moment, lit up, a blinking-open like a firefly, and then gone, changed back into a normal gray-black insect body vibrating lightly in the air.

I think now about how what he said had turned me transparent, for a moment, but only to him, and not to myself. I think now of the bareness of the unlit insect body, untethered, unseen, free.

One night, my mother makes braised short ribs for dinner. She tells us that she can never get them quite right, that she doesn't know what the secret was to my grandma's version. My grandma used to cook feasts on the regular. My grandpa used to take hundreds of family-gathering photos and edit with two VCRs hundreds of hours worth of home-video footage.

They don't do these things anymore, but still they seem ceaselessly happy. Even in the oldest photos of them that I've seen, they are already in their twenties and married. I am only able to imagine them from that point forward, their war-torn childhoods are nowhere to be seen.

&

It was time to leave the party. After five hours of inhaling invisible cat, my lungs felt scraped and hollow and my cough sounded like metal, and Alex's unwanted advances had proven too much, and Lana and I both desperately wanted out. For a while we seemed free, to leave to go back to Alex's place without him, and then suddenly, maybe brought about by one glimpse of a confused expression, one second of instability, one utterance of less-than-100% knowledge, Alex changed his mind. His mind, his pace, he was getting ready, putting on his jacket, there was no stopping him, despite all our protests and assurances, he was going to walk us home to his home, and whatever happened once that happened, I knew it wasn't going to be exciting. There was no way out.

We walked in silence, and then prepared to part ways with Sam. Hugs, lackluster farewells, I felt embarrassed for all of us, for finding ourselves in this situation, this version, in which not one person was promised a happy ending. Sam disappeared down into the entrance of the metro station, and we turned to continue on. But then suddenly Sam shouted back, was racing back up the steps, the metro gate was closed, it wasn't running after all, and in the next instant Lana was turning toward me, whispering about not really wanting to go back to Alex's place and how uncomfortable it was and in a crucial moment of chaos, a flurry, that single second when something can happen, when the window is slightly cracked open and things are free to fly in either direction, I said calmly, quickly, "Hey, it's a sign. I think we should go to the Eiffel Tower."

So we went. Alex came with us, but still we went. The journey was full of dazed silence, but we made it. We got out at the Trocadero stop on the opposite side of the Seine, walked up the stairs out of the station, and found ourselves having to go downhill, and up again, and everything was covered in trash and broken glass from New Year's revelry hours prior, but then, how high and solidly the tower rose, and how with even more certainty, it disappeared into the clouds.

Triptych Portrait With Doors In Closed Position

2016

THE ARTIST TELLS me to create a frame for my story. Be a master builder. Erect a steeple to the skies, supported by scaffolding that holds up a clearly defined, easily categorized shape. You can have just a beginning and just an end, but a middle, a core, cannot exist by itself. It's defined by what surrounds it, what comes before, what comes after. A frame for your story will make it more palatable. It will be easier for your reader, your listener, to hold, to stomach.

I nod. I like this idea, of my story being something that needed rearranging in order for people to stomach it. An unruly story that needs to be tamed, enclosed, subordinated. Put a frame around it, show people where to look, show people that it is worthy of consideration, if not admiration.

I ask if I should frame the story with a wedding. Weddings are ripe. Family, friends, strangers, social mores, traditions, every kind of relationship, food, alcohol, dancing, consumerism, money, everything comes into play. Or what about a gathering in a kitchen or around a dining table? Talking and storytelling while eating or preparing food. That seems right somehow, centering around the essential base need for sustenance and company. The artist shakes his head. He's more of a proponent of private, small-scale encounters. Mundane encounters with the known and unknown. Encounters with people and with other stimuli, like art. Stories that encounter other stories.

A story within a story within a story. Or, perhaps a triptych. I am more interested in a story on top of a story. A triptych painting kept folded shut.

I lie in bed between seven and ten p.m., looking out the window. I see a big bug, wonder for a second about the big bug, before it lights up. Fireflies outside my window. Nothing, light, nothing, light.

2046

In 2046, people would talk about how love used to be much slower. There would be time-lapse footage of a pale pink flower petal, unfurling itself in grainy slow-motion video, captions flashing across the bottom of the screen, saying just look at the wonder of life, look at the slowness of this woman, revealing herself. I'd have a job like researching old educational videos from the last century—most of them I'd be able to find digitized, though there'd be rumors of many that had been suppressed or "lost." It is worth the wait, the time-lapse video would drone on, sans serif yellow letters blaring at your eyes, peeling down your lower eyelids. It is worth it, it would menace, the pink petal uncurling to a wider curl, un-arcing, throwing, ever so slowly, itself, its soft belly, to the puncturing of your pupils.

People would talk about how there used to be events called speed dating, in which many men and many women sat in rows facing each other, and rotated, usually the men did, every five minutes, they scooted their bottoms over to the next seat, for a next date, with the next five-minute woman. There was a host, and a timer buzzer, and you took notes on notecards, so that you could remember your first impressions.

The ways we come together will always evolve. In tiny ways, in big ways. Take the artist, for instance. The artist and I met in such a humdrum way, and yet he was always trying to tell this very uneventful story of our meeting, and I'd have to stop him before he bored everyone to tears. This type of behavior has probably endured for hundreds of years. This is what I'd be thinking about, while in line for the weekend Turn-of-the-Millennia Throwback Movies event at the MoviePlex, a double marathon consisting of Wong Kar-wai's *Chungking Express* and *Fallen Angels*; and then *Days of Being Wild, In the Mood for Love,* and *2046.* Those movies were all about love, how it was never aligning quite right, even though we've been trying for eons. In the film *2046,* there's even a train that takes passengers to 2046, a place where everything always stays the same. You go there to recapture lost memories, maybe to relive past love, which remains forever steadfast in 2046. But even then, it still somehow manages not to align quite right. Even with a train that takes you straight there, sometimes you'd find yourself running in the opposite direction. It makes me happy to imagine where I would go, what or who I would visit, if I were to get on the train to 2046.

The man in front of me in line for movie tickets, wearing a blue sweater, would be trying to tear open the wrapper to his 72-Hour Wide Awake Energy Bar, rip it right down the middle seam, but it's not opening, and on one particularly forceful effort, the bar would fling out of his fingers and a plasticky thwack would hit him in the face, and he would jerk back, almost stumbling into me. I would barely move, lean my body back, just enough. Just enough so that we wouldn't touch.

2006

Gus and I met up near the bookstore. I'd wanted him to come meet me at the bookstore, when I finished my shift, partly so that he would meet my coworkers, or my coworkers would see him, just so that I could know, later on, that he was real. Someone else would know, that he was a real person, whom I knew, once. Otherwise, once he disappeared, I would never know for sure. On the way to get something to eat, we stopped by my apartment. He stood in the middle of my room. I was not used to other people in my room—it happened so infrequently I could count recent occasions on one hand. He was tall, he was wearing many things, a hat, shoes, a jacket, a belt, a sweater, other layers, a watch maybe, a wedding ring. What are the handcuffs for, Celine? Halloween costume, I said, and continued with my story about small talk, or it may have been just small talk.

I was not okay. I was not okay, I had asked him, after many iterations and ideas and scenarios in my head, if we could meet and talk, with the understanding that something had been wreaked, something might be irretrievable. But the understandings you come to, by yourself, in your head, with nobody else weighing in, sometimes they only have traction in the confines of your head. His surprise at my seriousness relieved me. Sure, he had said, are you okay??, he had said, with the wondrous shock of many question marks, and this relieved me too. Oh, I said, phew, I thought.

2046

In 2046 I would take a "Pre-Modern" drawing class at the Humanities Center, which would be next to the MoviePlex in the strip mall shopper-tainmentplex. Sandwiched between the Center and the Plex would be a boba shop, called Boba-Go-Banana.

In my drawing class, we would do left-brain exercises in which you had to write the answer to questions using your non-dominant hand. The question would be, Where do you see yourself in five years? Using my left hand, I'd scrawl some general answer about doing something creative with my life, and then I'd write, as a sort of addendum: I better not still be fucking thinking about this guy in five years, that's for sure. I'd feel a small thrill, writing that with my wrong hand, in that strange subversive scrawl, *fucking*. Although perhaps the more terrifying thrill would be that I had lied, in this meaningless art class exercise, to myself. There would be no *this guy*. I wouldn't be close to anybody. The closest I'd come to people would be as an apparition staring longingly at the knit pattern on someone's intarsia sweater. Once there had been the possibility of the artist, but he was not seriously in the picture, who was I fucking kidding?

&

My mother would've been one of the pioneers of the Red (Con)Tent method, teaching women the world over how to compartmentalize their periods. She would lead workshops in this, a kind of guided meditation toward bento-box-like separations. As a girl, she would've taught me that I'd need to have my periods outside of time, in RagTime/BloodWave time, a zone that didn't waste the time of men. It gave you this twinned self, you'd get to exist in another compartment simultaneously—a body-&-blood zone. This would've been considered, at one time, a kind of kooky hookey hokey mumbo jumbo hippie dippie new age way of going about things. But after the popularity of IUDs diminished over time, it would've become the accepted norm. My mother would've made a lot of money off the books and comprehensive guides she'd written. I would've recently gone rogue though, gone back to having my periods. Back-to-the-landers, but back to the body.

2016

After work, I get home, open the door to my bedroom, close it behind me, kick out of my shoes, drop my purse and jacket onto the couch. I click off the light switch. It feels cooler in the room when it's dark. An optical illusion, a synaesthetic delusion. Tricking your mind is half the battle. Probably more. I lie down on top of the bed. I am waiting desperately for my period to be over so that I can masturbate without getting blood all over my hands. It is enough having to deal with the absolutely necessary aspects of bloodletting—pulling on the string to extricate the sodden red tampon, carefully dropping it into the toilet bowl, carefully making sure it doesn't swing erratically or touch anything. Unwrapping a new tampon, placing the pads of my thumb and index fingers on the finger grips of the applicator while pushing it in, pushing in the actual swab of tampon, pulling back out the applicator, sometimes bloody, like a syringe, slipping it bloodily back into the torn wrapper, throwing it away. How many moments of getting blood on your hands, the dreading dragging tiny fear of splattering, of bloodying clothing or rug or towel. Plug that shit up. Put a cork in it. Staunch the wound. Do whatever you have to do, to stop it.

Some women have debilitating periods. Some of them accept this, as a fact, period. Period. This is your life, period. Some of them continue to seek solace, in new medications, new doctors, new pills, new lights (won't you see it, in a new light?), new exercises, new diets, new surgeries, new alternative holistic crystals, homeopathic remedies, poultices that smell like prickly pear. Be the change you can see, some man said. This is, once a month, the only change you can see, the only thing, a huge red splotch in your line of vision, the smear of blood dashed across your car window, and no matter where you steer the wheel, or how fast you force the windshield wiper blades, everything is red. All roads lead to blood.

Long ago, with my first boyfriend Gus, we fought a lot. He used to mark my upcoming period days on his calendar, months in advance, but I think he actually provoked me more near the red-marked dates. You have no idea what this is like, I would say, feeling out of control, to become a walking wound every month, to bleed this way, to feel like your person becomes defined by its relation to a fucking bloody, bleeding orifice, to have blood smeared on the insides of your upper thighs, to feel this bloody wetness, to be draining yourself of blood like this, to become inured to the sight of yourself bleeding. I hated being on my period, was relieved at the first sight of blood, but every moment after the first sight was so unpretty. The heaviness, the wetness, the sweatiness of having a plastic pad, the sounds of plastic wrappers, the dryness of tampon absorption, wiping blood, the blatant redness of the smear on toilet paper boring a hole into my eyes.

&

The artist likes his beef cooked medium, he likes me bloody. Doesn't mind me bloody. I am less than racked, but still confronted with feelings of guilt. Blood guilt. Rag guilt. Unsure. This requires additional layers of uncertainty, questioning, attempts at predicting, understanding. Do I tell him before agreeing to meet up that I'm on my period? Is that incredibly presumptuous or incredibly unnecessary? Or just slightly one or the other?

He gives me a toothbrush, a small towel. We go to bed, what's the matter, he asks, when I squirm out of the way when he reaches down into my shorts. I'm on my period. *I'm on my period.* An apology, a groan, a half laugh. Contrition, a request for forgiveness. Forgive me for my blood. Excuse me for my mess.

He says something like, so? or That's okay. I say something like I don't want to bleed all over your sheets. Gus once said it looked like we had killed a squirrel in our bed. Or I don't mind, maybe that's what the artist is saying. I remind myself that this all makes sense. He's an artist, he's lived with women before sometimes in shacks in the woods for years. I say, I have nowhere to put my tampon, he tells me just to put it in his T-shirt, I am shocked. I would rather not be shocked all the time—I tell myself this is great. It's dark, we're on his lofted bed, here, yeah, just put it in here, doesn't matter, I'll just wash it. I shrug a small shrug, in the dark, yank out the tampon, place it in the folds of the T-shirt he is holding out.

Was there blood everywhere, I ask later. Am I hoping for blood? The artist is coming back into the room from the bathroom. No, he says, but I definitely had to wash my mouth out with Listerine. I don't know what else to do but laugh, a laugh of astonishment, open-mouthed chagrin. The taste of blood in your mouth.

I wake up sweating, another heat-wave wake-up call, and reach over to the table to grab a glass of water. I open the door to the bedroom. In the hallway to the rest of the apartment, there floats a strip of spotlit dust motes, in the beam of light shining in from the bathroom window. It's above eye level, and I stare up at the specks. I breathe deeper, inhale more dust, everyone is inhaling all of this dust all the time. Specks of bodies.

&

When I receive a copy of Gus and Slayde's wedding film, I have just had a long restless day of nothing. It is my first day off in two weeks, a Monday, and what I did was this: woke up. Noted the deflated nature of my inflatable mattress. Took a shower. Ate cereal and blackberries for breakfast. Went to the bank to get cash for rent. Ate a left-over sandwich from the afternoon prior, reheated questionably on the stove in a wok, on low heat. Read a little, wrote a little. Discovered the hole in the inflatable mattress. Ordered a patch-up kit online. Went to the drugstore and bought some black tights and two cans of soup.

I watch the wedding video while eating Chickarina canned soup—the voice-overs of family speeches and toasts overlaying shots of the bride getting her makeup done, the groomsmen at the barbershop. I watch it twice. The third time, I stop it, before it gets to the part with Gus tying his tie and shoelaces, in slow motion.

2006

One summer toward the end of college, I moved in, just for six months, into the house Gus lived in. It was probably July, and L.A. was hot and dusty. It was hot at seven in the morning, it was hot at seven at night. Dusty because of desert dirt, dusty because of the construction sites that were always outside of whatever window through which you were staring.

I moved in, next door. A few turgid and warm summer months leading into some mild and windy fall and winter days, over those creaky hardwood floors, and then I would be gone to study abroad. But for now, this was what it was. Gus moved my mattress for me. Hefted it to one side, walked up the sidewalk with it, sixty feet away, to my new house. He was shirtless, wearing shorts, flip-flops. His body was Roman-statue perfect, but he carried himself as if he were heavier, stomping, hulking, ungraceful, clumsy. Then back, and back again, with my box spring.

I was skirting a wide gaping hole of pre-graduation angst and uncertainty, and living in that big dark house was some sort of perfect backdrop to it all. The entire complex of houses was a sunken forest in the middle of the street, swarming darkly with vegans, bisexuals, hippies, rock stars, skateboarders, and graffiti artists, and then, them. Or, us.

There was always that Astroturf walkway, dividing the two sides of the bunch of houses, and you could tell it was a bright green a long time ago, but now it was blotchy and dark, and most of the time when you crossed that walkway, it was soggy. The front door was almost never locked. At night, at the table in the corner of the living room, Gus and I sometimes sat side by side, reading or writing, with just one small lamp on the table spreading out its light, the rest of the rooms dark and still.

When the small slew of strange summer subletters started coming through, each staying only a few weeks at a time, Gus and I watched them, idly guessing about their comings and goings. We especially liked the first roommate—Albert. We talked fondly about his odd mannerisms, perhaps because he fit in so awkwardly with the rest of us, and smiled proudly when we discussed his predilection for trance music and hookah bars. We waited up for him, and worried when it was late and he still hadn't returned home.

I tried to organize that summer into a nice orderly chronology later on, but always failed. While I lay in bed, staring at the small oblong poster on the ceiling, I tried, but I realized I couldn't remember eating at all that summer and fall. Those months were filled with that house, and those streets, but what did we eat? What was in the refrigerator, the pantry, the cabinets? It seemed like we all miraculously floated on through, surviving on the odd handful of sour candy or bite of blood orange.

Once, we bought a watermelon and tried to fill it with vodka, but became confused. Philippe, from Austria, was living with us at that time,

Philippe, with his white blonde hair, and elfin face, who always walked around in a red silk robe. Gus and I sliced off the top of the watermelon, and started pouring the vodka in, but it was absorbing too slowly, so Philippe gave the melon a few stabs. The three of us ended up feeding it the vodka slowly, over a couple of days, like a cranky baby we were nursing around the clock.

Most of that summer, we just watched movies, or read, one or two or three of us at a time. It was like being in some other universe, the bamboo blinds moving slightly in the windows at night, the sound of crickets outside, and the bunch of us in there, disparate orphans, speaking sleepily or energetically about art and politics and school and books and drugs and films.

On occasion, we ventured out, usually late at night, and strolled in the aisles of the twenty-four-hour drugstore, or hung out at Penny Lane, searching for the few movies left in the foreign section we hadn't yet rented. Sometimes we went to Ralphs, sometimes we struggled over the fence and into the cemetery.

I left at the end of September. We lit sparklers left over from the fourth of July in the driveway, and I hugged everyone goodbye. I'd write postcards, and emails, and I'd be back soon enough, I promised. And I came back. There had been an earthquake while I was away, but I came back.

We were having a dinner that Sunday after my return. I set the table. Slayde was coming up to eat with us, this dinner. I didn't say anything to anyone, about this. Nobody said anything. We went to the store, and cooked, and moved things around, as if we were a normal family of friends, getting ready for a normal dinner. I was looking forward to it, I realized, to the actual dinner, sitting there at that table, in the lamplit evening, close together, so that I could watch her interacting with him, but also with everyone else. So that I could watch her and feel condescension about who she was, and what they were, and how she did not fit in with us, how she was not one of us, how she was intruding on our family. I felt calm, I didn't feel anything.

2016

He's an artist. I say this to my friends, by way of explanation, by way of the last ditch, by way of being merciful—turn on the fountain, turn on the water, and suddenly the fountain makes sense.

Before I said this, I could see in their restless trembling eyeballs, that nothing made sense. But that they would let it slide. I don't want to let it slide, so I give them the thing that will connect the dots.

The artist sends me a message that ends in an ellipsis, only instead of three dots, it's three commas. I cannot fathom how someone can function like this.

I think about the artist while I masturbate. I slide under the covers, the covers being an empty duvet cover, in my jeans, it feels dirty to be doing this. Inside the bed is supposed to be clean, only for pajamas, flannel, matching top and bottoms. Peter Pan collar. Not for denim, which harbors in its tiny ridges all the dirt of the day, like macaroni pasta harboring hidden reserves of cheese. You never know what you might find. Surprises and secrets.

I slide shut the window. It's only October, but it's cold. Crisp is a euphemism for cold. Masturbate is a euphemism for breach, alone. My fingers are cold. My toes are cold. Insides are still warm. Even a dead body will hold warm wetness, for a while.

I wash my hands, soaping especially the middle fingers on my right hand. I look at my face in the mirror. My cheeks look a little pink—from what? An unvigorous walk? A cigarette? Espresso? A blush signifying residual shame, or intensity of something, from having almost wept over the cop in *Chungking Express*, forlornly telling his towel, "You're a real disappointment to me."?

Once, the artist asked me, don't you want to touch me? I didn't want to, then. Or, I thought by not touching him, I was staying shy of crossing a certain boundary, I was not-crossing a certain line, I was refraining for his sake. I could be cold, I could be crisp, I could sing songs in a light, airy voice while working behind a snack bar counter and feel nothing.

I wake up in the morning, and look at the thermometer on my night-stand. Fifty degrees. In my bedroom. I eat all my meals at the coffee table and couch in my living room. I eat all my meals at knee level. Below, knee level, really; I know this because the coffee table hits my shins right below my knees. My bowl of boiling hot oatmeal cools completely in two minutes.

2006

Somewhere recently, grafitti on the side of a building, someone had writ-ten: it's simple—if you want to be seen, show yourself. If you want to be understood, explain yourself.

Was that stupid or smart? Neither. Meaningless.

2046

The day after the movie marathon night, I would meet my parents for dinner. They would express worry, as usual, about me being alone. It's good to have someone, my mom would say. Someone who's in your life, a lot. Someone who lives not too far away. Soon all of your friends will be married and with kids, and with families of their own... Well, you'll see.

I would refrain from saying anything, except uh huh. What else is there to say? Yes, I am fucked.

Or, should I say, actually, well, there is someone. There is someone who would notice. The artist, who's resurfaced in my life, would notice. If you must do something as conventional as scorekeeping, then yes, I suppose you would conclude that I talk to this person everyday. But I cannot tell my mother this, I cannot tell him this, I can barely even tell myself this.

It does not soothe me, or reassure me, that friendship can be this wide open and lenient. I had not wished for this, for this demonstration that friendships—relationships—could be so pliable, so shapeless, so prone to stretching in all directions.

2006

Gus and I ventured out of my bedroom, into the living room. The apartment was empty except for us, and we were both in our underwear—he was wearing boxers, everyone wore those boxer shorts then; I was wearing an old undershirt tank top and underwear. We needed water. It was hot. He pulled open the screen door, and we stepped onto the grimy floor of the balcony to look down at Sunset Blvd. rushing beneath us. The sun had not quite set yet, but its intentions were clear. If someone down there looked up and saw me, they might think I was completely naked, he said, kicking at the bumpy cement wall of the balcony, that stopped at his ribs. We grinned at each other. He walked back inside, into the dimness of the living room, and we danced, swaying for several moments. While I poured another glass of water, he walked over to the barstool, where he had left his phone. I walked back out to the balcony, and watched him from outside. He put the phone up to his ear, expressionless, then serious. He looked up, met my eyes. As much as part of me started sinking, another part of me started to feel like I was floating—either way, I forgot about breathing. I walked inside, he looked panicked, turned away from me, walked into the kitchen, his voice low and I heard fast words, I'm okay, I'm okay, yeah, yeah, I'll be back. I looked over at the coffee table. There were a whole bunch of red Netflix envelopes scattered on top, Strunk and White's *The Elements of Style*, Eileen Chang's *Lust, Caution*. He was walking back now, calm. I had about sixteen missed calls from my brother and then my parents since yesterday afternoon, he said quietly. I looked at him and waited. I have to go, he said, they were really worried, they called the cops. What, I interrupted. He looked down, My brother thought I would come home yesterday. I mean, I was supposed to go home. He's not used to—He stopped. I don't know what to say. And Slayde, she flew back to surprise me. I have to go, he said. I nodded. We kissed, behind the building, by his car.

2016

When I look back to that moment behind the building, by his car, I think to myself, yes, that was the kind when you know it's the last time.

2046

While I wait in line, I would think about this speed dating thing—the concept of it would seem very antiquated, but also strangely futuristic, like something we should be doing now. Fast, forward. A little bit like an over-the-top version of the future, as envisioned by people from back in the 1990s, when they had no idea what it would be like. Oh, are you feeling like love is too slow? Fear not, my lonely ladies and gentlemen! Try this new-fangled dating method we've transported straight from the future: SPEED DATING!

I would keep staring at the dark blue weave of the sweater on the man in front of me. Intarsia. I'd be really into this word, intarsia, because of its old-fashioned sound—it's a word used for knitting and woodwork after all. Although in 2046 it'd also happen to be the name of a very popular over-the-counter psychostimulant. I would stare into the wayward fibers, really into them, into the dust and the knit and the wool and the motes and mites. I would think about how this man in the sweater who could not open his energy bar wrapper appropriately could be the love of my life.

Once, they say, people wrote love letters. It only counted as love if the love was not there anymore. It only counted as love letters if the letters were all that was left. There was love, war, and afterwards, letters floated like debris, back to the ground. Nothing was around. There was nothing left, nothing but a very thin air.

2016

Gus used to write me letters from his shared recording studio space at The Brewery, on the nights when he stayed late, when he was there long enough to take a break to eat a sandwich, and write me a letter.

I'm back in Orange County for a funeral. I'm there for a week, cleaning out my old closets at my parents' house, and boxing up some things to take back to my new place in Echo Park. I find the letters at the bottom of a box labeled CONTENTS: DISCONTENTS, and I read them, imagining him on his cracked leather stool. I do not care to count how many years later it is.

Dear Celine,

I arrived home this evening and the house was full of people. My brother's band had been recording, and everyone was still hanging around, drinking beers, leaning against walls, seated on the couch, boots propped up on the coffee table. It was loud, din, laughing, it was hot inside the house, and I was supposed to be talking to Peter about a new project we are doing together, but all I could think about was you, and so I excused myself, and went to my room, and sat at my desk, and decided to write to you. You are at work now, and I wanted you to have this, to read, when you got home. It was only here, the rest of the sounds and the rest of the world stumbling loudly forward in the other rooms, sounds made dim by my closed doors, and the walls, that I felt happy, that I felt quiet and happy and that was because I could think, which meant I could think about you.

It is difficult for me to think about what this means. Everything here in this house is my life. My brother, his friends, who have become my friends, the work they are doing, the work I have started in collaboration with them, everything I have been creating for myself for the past three years. My weekends are regular, the time spent with my brother, running with him, our drives into the desert, hauling out all of our sound and recording equipment and instruments, the smell of the saguaros and the Joshua trees, the dry heat of the wind when we are on the 10 and the 62 with the windows cranked down. Coming home to this is what I have made for myself, something I have consciously created, this space, the ability to have this to come home to. People to make music with, to make art with, to put on shows with, to talk with about sound synthesis theory over an endless parade of watery Tecates.

It's not something I can dismiss, or put aside. It's important to my life—for what it is, it is *my life. I am tied to this, to my family, not just to my brother, but to my parents for whom I have caused grief and for whom this, finally, is something they do not have to worry about and make sacrifices over. Slayde, too, is a part of all this. She has taught me so much, she has given me so much, of herself, of her life, her friends and relationships, her support and guidance, she has shared this world with me, given it to me.*

And yet, now, this.

It is unfair. We talk about this, you and I, this notion of fairness, of deserving, who gets what, for what? I've made myself a sandwich, to escape the party, to take into my room here with me, while I write to you, and I look at it on the plate, and I only understand that you are right, that nobody deserves anything, nobody has a right, intrinsically, to anything, we place these importances as we see fit, according to our own feelings. But, here, I want to do what is right. I want there to be something that is undeniably right, and when I think about this, all I think is Celine Celine Celine.

Here. This word implies a world, where there is me (I'm here), there is you (wherever you are, you're not here), and there is a space between us. To echo your earlier "postcard moment," I wish you were here. I wish we were in some house, some building, even if not in the same room, just in the same building somewhere, where I knew you were in the next room, where I knew we could be in the same room, even if just to sit, or stand, breathing, not saying anything, not touching, just near each other.

I'll end here for now. I'll see you soon. Monday?

Gus

2046

That's one. Love letter, I would mouth to myself, standing there in line. I would read it to myself, once, twice. It would take my breath away, did people really think like this, write like this? Letters with so little to hold onto, with so few tangible objects? Boots, coffee table, saguaro, sandwich, plate.

Here. Now. These are deictic words, as the artist once explained to me, which only accrue their meaning given contextual information. The artist and I had talked about this excitedly once, the idea of linguistic fulfillment or lack of fulfillment, language that could not be wholly complete or functional on its own. I had declared it an incompetence of language, a codependence. But the artist had deemed it symbiotic.

I'd have to wrench myself out of the memory and focus back on staring at the man's back. Could I, as a person, experience deixis? You're a real disappointment to me, I'd try whispering to the man's sweater. But it wouldn't feel right. I'd try again. Are you my context? I'd ask. I'd mouth to the man's back, would you give me meaning? I'd maybe edge just a little bit closer, until my face was just about to touch. All of the wool knit fibers and body dust and motes and mites. Specks of my body touching specks of his body.

The Forecast

BEFORE BEE FELL asleep on Sunday night, she did what she usually did, which was lie down on her back in the center of her bed, straight and symmetrical, push her shoulder blades down and back a little bit for better posture, and make several small movements as if to straighten her pillow, which most likely was already pretty straight, considering the fastidious manner in which she made her bed in the mornings. Once she'd closed her eyes and breathed in and out, evenly, three times, she turned her mind to what she would wear in the morning.

Neither her direct supervisor, the Editor, nor the founder-president Mr. Haussmann, had ever indicated in the least way they noticed what she wore to work. Bee just thought about the next day's outfit as a way to simultaneously do something practical and also put herself to sleep. She would see in her mind all the socks she had stuffed into the top drawer, and then narrow down by how cold or hot it might be the next day, and if it might rain, and what shoes she might be wearing, in accordance to temperature or precipitation. Next, she would imagine what pants she had. It was going to be Monday, so she needn't think about wearing the same pants two days in a row to the office. There were only four pairs of sweatpants to pick from anyway. Then, keeping in mind the cut, color, and waist of the pants, she would decide what would go on top. Tops were in the second drawer from the bottom. She would not wear a dark gray T-shirt with light gray sweatpants, for instance. Maybe the white button-down shirt. She would think of a hooded sweatshirt, maybe, but by then, it was such an uninvigorating task that she would already be asleep.

From a blank and stone-cold sleep, Bee woke up Monday morning on her stomach. She woke up on her stomach only when she had bad sleep, which caused her to roll onto her stomach in order to protect the soft white flesh of the front of her body. Twisting her neck, she looked up and around to her back, and saw that the blanket lay perfectly straight and flat over her, so smooth and neat that aside from making the one roll over onto her stomach at some point, she must have lain the whole night as still as if she were dead.

She looked out the window at the sun, bright, but neutral behind brick and glass and insulation. She looked at the branches of the tree, which gave no sign of budding. She pulled open and pushed closed the drawers she needed, to get her socks and underwear and shirt and pants. She walked out into the kitchen and down the hallway, and turned out into the other hallway, and opened and shut three consecutive doors, finally locking the outermost one behind her. Outside in the slight morning wind, she turned right up the hill on her street, before turning back around once she remembered she had parked on the bottom of the hill the afternoon before.

At the first turn, she forgot to signal. She signaled after she had already made the turn. This was unusual, and not part of the routine. But she got back on track. She would not be veering from her usual habits, just because of some error of forgetfulness. Do not hesitate. Do not wait for anything, or anyone. Do not succumb to distractions. She turned on the radio to the morning radio station she liked mostly for the elegant Continental accent of the host. Then she stayed in the left lane until she passed the huge billboard for the Citadel Outlets, which marked approximately one-third of her commute down this three-lane boulevard, at which point she merged into the middle lane, remembering to signal, and then she caught sight of the corner of the sign indicating the west-bound freeway on-ramp, which was her cue to merge into the right lane.

The office was precariously nestled into a slightly elevated lump of a lot built into the side of the freeway entrance; the production warehouse was semi-attached and stretched out behind the back of the office building, seeming to tunnel itself into a cavernous hole that must have been gouging into the underside of the freeway ramp. Bee flipped up her turn signal to show she was turning right. Nobody else in the long lines of cars ahead and behind her, or the two lanes of cars lined up bumper-to-bumper to her left, ever turned into this place. They probably thought she had left her turn signal on too long, from merging to the right before, or had meant to indicate she was about to turn right onto the freeway on-entrance, maybe, and changed her mind, or that it was a mistake. But it was correct. She had a right to turn in here, she worked here.

She parked her car in the third space on the right side of the slanted angle lot, yanking back on her parking brake. The Design Director's sports-car was two spaces down, gleaming and black, like a panther's lowered head. Bee opened the door on the right side of the building. She walked past the two orange armchairs and the orange bench flanking the aspidistra and pothos and sansevieria plants with their unbearably dusty leaves. This arrangement must have formerly functioned as a sort of waiting area, when there were once celebrity visitors, stars inquiring about stars. An alcove off the left side of this area led to the restroom, a clean but dim room, covered in mustard yellow tiles. On the back of the toilet was a neat pile of fifteen-year-old nudie magazines. Continuing on down the main hallway, the first door to the right was usually closed. Up until one year before Bee had started carrying out her days at the compound, this room—with the wood sheeting on its door always looking brown and reticent—had belonged to the Marketing Director's older brother, who had been the Production Director. He had died. The Marketing Director worked on the other side of the office, the left side, with the Office Manager and the Head of Circulation. The dead Production Director had never been replaced, and Bee had never directly asked or spoken—or been spoken to directly—about him, not once after the office tour on her first day when the Editor had said to her, "This used to be the Production Director's office. He was the brother of the Marketing Director. He passed away one year ago. One year ago, today."

The next door down the hallway on the right side was Bee's door. There was her desk, L-shaped, upon which landed, sometimes, termite wings.

Sometimes, these very same termite wings fluttered up when she walked by, stirred up by the slightest movement in the air. Gray disembodied wings, the little termite ant bodies would never catch up to these airborne wings, the little termite ant bodies were probably trod upon and ground into the carpet. Behind the desk, there was a swiveling desk chair. Many hours were spent swiveling in this desk chair, not quite as many hours were spent rolling in the desk chair, as the vinyl office chair mat had cracked and sunken beneath the combined years of wear and weight of the last Editorial Assistant who labored in this room. The little grippers on the underside of the chair mat gripped on, however—tiny plastic bumps of teeth gnawing ineffectually at the carpet, a coarse mottle of avocado, harvest gold, and burnt orange fibers. Behind the desk there was one large bookshelf and two locked filing cabinets, and to the left of the desk, a lower bookshelf with a spider plant sitting on top of it. That wall, shared with the next office over, had a rectangular panel of frosted glass in it, so that if the Editor in her office next door moved into the right spot, Bee could see a slight hovering movement of her silhouette.

On her desk, she had a twelve-year-old laptop, three inches thick with a built-in trackball. This twelve-year-old laptop had no internet or printing capabilities—Bee had been instructed to use it to take notes. For internet or printing, she walked across the hall to the room directly opposite, the one with one wall of windows into the hallway, one wall of dry erase white board, one huge desktop computer, one fax machine, one printer, and also the machine that powered the forecast calculator, which looked like a huge version of the hygrothermograph machines in the corners of museums and art galleries. The monthly forecasts and numerology reports were faxed in by the Astrologer, by the first week of the month if they were lucky. And for specific individuals or occasions, the Editor would run astrological charts on the software housed in the desktop computer—before interviewing a prospective job applicant, for instance, or when venturing forth with a risky new business investment. The forecast calculator, then, was for the astrological miscellaney that fell in between those two bases. Whenever

Bee had spent a long day in the computer-and-other-machines room, she left with a headache—the machine powering the forecast calculator, especially, buzzed incessantly with a robust and self-important drone. It was not to be turned off.

And so, when at the end of the day that Monday, Bee walked all the way down the hallway to the room at the very end, she was only seeing in her mind a big, clean, round, white plate, and on the plate, a pile of green lentils, perfectly diced cubes of salty ham hock, all of it not touching the sides of the plate, but resting peacefully in the middle. She pulled her time card out of its slot, slipped it in between the jaws of the time clock machine. She waited, it took a moment, until she heard and felt the sharp metal clong of the punch. She walked back down the hallway towards the front of the building. She went back into her office to get her bag from the chair on the side, and saw that the Editor had left her the galley proofs to look over. Her desk was already piled with the card file boxes she had been working on during the day, so she brought the stack of sheets over to the dead Production Director's room in the next office over, where she sometimes did work that needed spreading out and a clean, quiet, empty space.

Bee was in the middle of proofing the French edition—everyone else had already left the office and gone home while she was doing the Spanish edition—when the phone rang. She looked at the thin gold hands of the clock on the wall. It was late, but not so late that she wouldn't be expected to pick up the phone. The voice on the other line came in gradually, as if from afar, as if getting closer. Hello, the voice said. It was a man's voice, deep and insistent. Hello, is this the Production Director? No, Bee said. No, this is not. Well, the man's voice said. Well. He helps me with this, sometimes. I need you to look up something for me. Um, Bee said. This is a privately-owned business, a publishing company. I know, the man's voice said. But he helps me with this, sometimes. It's not too difficult, is it, I just need you to look up a word for me. Pardon me? Bee said. If you want a forecast done, I can take a message. No, no, the man's voice said. I just need you to look up a word for me. A word? Bee said. Yes, the man's voice said. Sometimes, I hear a word I don't know, and since I don't know it, I don't know how to spell it. Huh, Bee said. And, continued the man's voice, since I don't know how to spell it, I can't look it up myself in my dictionary. Oh, Bee said. Oh. Could you please just look it up, the man's voice said. The Production Director used to do it for me. You can just look it up on a computer there, right? Okay, Bee said. Fine, she said. She turned over to the desktop computer on the small table on the side of the office, she woke it up, and opened up an online dictionary. What is the word? she asked. I just heard it on a radio show just now, the man's voice said. It's a very interesting word, and I don't know how to spell it. Okay, Bee said. Could you please tell me what the word is? I need to know what the word is, if I am going to look it up for you. I am ready to look up this word for you, she said. Again. She was adding more sentences to this conversation. She was in a hurry. She wanted to finish this, she wanted to get this over with.

She clamped the phone down between her right ear and the top of her shoulder, fingers poised over the keyboard, ready to type. Okay, the man's voice said finally. The word is

Peregrine.

Peregrine.

Peregrine? Bee said. Yes, the man's voice said, I think it was Peregrine Fal—

Right, Bee said, turning back to her galley proofs, and began spelling it out to him, P-E-R-E-G-R-I-N-E. Oh! the man's voice said. Oh, you know it? Wait.

No, Bee said to the man's voice. No. But she waited. She had not known she would. She had not thought she would. But she did. She had never noticed how that word, *peregrine*, sounded. Like it could be an exotic place, but also like a scientific name, or a mathematical shape. It sounded mild and gentle, but also menacing, exciting, full of blood. She felt like she could feel her own blood moving, following her own body, which seemed also to be forming into a certain shape.

The man's voice was saying something more, a murmur. She waited for him to grasp hold of his pen, and press its tip into paper. She spelled it again, slow, for the man with no internet, who could not look up the meaning of a word because he did not know how to spell it. She waited for him to catch up. She looked like she was just sitting there, in a chair, in an office, but inside, she could have been moving, so, so fast.

Desert Dreams Are Always In Green

THERE WERE FACTS I already knew, when I met him in Marseille. His wife was living in L.A. She'd just finished studying art/experimental sound/ video installation at Cal Arts, and worked at a cafe. She didn't like driving, and took the bus everywhere. She had been one of the first American Apparel models, an early favorite, luridly pale buttocks straining against bright, restless cotton on Sunset Boulevard billboards.

He knew my sister, Beatrice, first. They're both photographers. They only vaguely knew each other, which is saying something, because Beatrice doesn't really do vague. Everyone loves her, but somehow Wade wasn't fooled. I like to think this meant something, but it doesn't have to. Extraordinary beginnings don't necessarily beget extraordinary endings.

His wife was a good deal younger than him, and when they got married, five years ago, she was very young—nineteen to Wade's thirty-one. Helen had been born in Chengdu, but had moved to L.A. with her oceanographer father when she was seven. That's where she and Beatrice became friends. In a rather odd turn of events, but really, not so odd for our family, Beatrice had been sent to the West Coast for some regulatory boarding school. She always says that she immediately felt natural there, a regular chainsmoking wildflower cowboy. Even though it was L.A., and not Wyoming or anything.

Wade showed me photographs of Helen, black and white, but in my mind, I already knew her in color from those ads. She gazed down at the spindly tops of palm trees, eyes giving away nothing, stoic. Eyes like a blank white wall, begging to be defaced. From those billboards, I imagined, fancifully, that in her blood ran equally the Mongolian savagery of Genghis Khan and the implacable, unimpeachable wisdom of Confucius. Her mouth was a plumply turgid hexagon, always tainted red and dry like stained wood chips, her long black hair a cloud of unfettered motion, flying.

In high school and college, Wade had been a football player and also an acid dealer, and he showed me photos of those days too, in between trading stories about L.A., telling me about what it was like to not live in the same city as Helen, and showing me, step by step, how he was making the bouillabaisse. We'd recognized each other at a mutual friend's wedding, which had been a weeklong project just outside of Marseille, and now, finished with it, I had found myself invited to Wade's family's apartment in the city, the city of blue. I sat at that table in his kitchen, mouthing tiny sips of a Cointreau cocktail.

I'd been moving around for months, probably a year. I had stared out so many moving vehicles, waited interminably for so many rides and flights, I thought I could no longer stop myself from looking through people, from looking and revealing nothing, as Helen seemed to do from those billboards, from drawing closed a third eyelid like a lizard, clear but soundproof. Nictitating, I repeated, over and over in my head. The way it got caught up in my throat and mouth.

There inside that apartment in Marseille, though, I could not keep my heartbeats still, my eyes were swiveling wildly, I had never wanted to be so attentive, to absorb so wholly, sitting and watching and listening to someone who seemed to know so many useful, practical things that I didn't know. Someone who had a life I was hungering for. There were objects to Wade's life that had weight, heavy things, not the theoretical dust of Foucault, Barthes, Deleuze, Derrida, who floated through my research, but real, fleshy things, pronouncements about love and cities, solid words in the kitchen air and a knife against a vegetable's green waxy skin, and generous ways to move around and talk to a guest like me, that would be warm, and familiar.

Years before, Beatrice and I had spent a summer together in Europe. That was the summer of inhuman heat, prehistoric heat, when all the elderly in London and Paris were crumpling and dying in their tiny apartments, while the rest of the family went south for their August vacations. I took three ice-cold showers per day that summer. This, this wasn't the same.

There, inside that apartment in Marseille, the air conditioner coolly dried our sweat. Outside, it was warm and windy. The sky had the glowing gray opaqueness of a moonstone shifting under a changing lightscape.

I stood up from the bed and looked out the window. People below on the street held umbrellas, and ice cream cones.

&

What is it like, to have someone say they want to see you? What is it like, to say this is not unusual for you, but this is unusual for me?

What is it like, to say you are not in danger, and not to say, that I am.

I suppose you choose one or the other. Someone for whom words stay inside. Or someone for whom words come easily—flattery, charm, mouth spilling with: you're so cute, you're very sexy. Someone who finds so many women beautiful and tells them so. Someone who says you have such beautiful skin, you have such beautiful hair, you have such pretty legs, I love your hands, everything is beautiful, beautiful eyelashes, beautiful thighs, beautiful hips, a beautiful laugh out of beautiful lips. You don't question it, you know he means it, he believes it, but he believes, fervently, so many things, for so many women, that even if it's sincere, it's not as valuable, not as precious.

Still, you are a beggar.

Still, you think, it is nice to have someone who wants to take care of you, look after you, flatter you, touch you, talk to you, pay attention to you, spend time with you.

Still, you think.

Still.

I think about whether after spending time with him, I feel better, or worse. Better or worse?

It should be so simple. It should be such a straight line. It should be so black, and so white.

§

At the beginning, each time I assembled her, got her set up in my mind, I wasn't sure which would upset me less: if she were just like me, or nothing like me. I ended up making her nothing like me, because I knew if I tried to recreate her as just like me, she'd still somehow end up just slightly better. Just like me but with shinier eyes. So instead, I went with the opposite—I put her at home, while I escaped. She stayed at home, while I took in the world.

There are facts I already knew, and there are scenes I saw. There are the private moments I imagined, when they first met:

All of these events, the events that would eventually transpire, respire again, again, sprouted from this one tiny folding, unfolding. A bend, a crease, one sheaf doubled over, sheets and leaves, collapse.

It is a Monday in February. You brush your fingertips over something on Heliotrope Drive, after stepping off the bus. Red, wet paint sign. It is sticky. You stare, consternation, at the faint streaks on your fingertips.

Something is happening.

You are dry. Unwell. Winter skin, winter mind. Encased, becoming a blur, edges fuzzing into the atmosphere. Undifferentiated. Becoming the sky, the air.

The sky that evening is pressing itself far from the earth. Inaccessible. Distant. Cold. Bright mackerel clouds spreading thin, like butter skidding evenly uneven across the bumpy crevices of dry toast.

It wants nothing to do with you. It wants nothing to do with this. Cold shoulder. Indifferent.

Some things had already been happening. Mercury was in retrograde. You had spilled a Diet Coke all over a baby's face the week before. It may or may not have had something to do with the jostling for room in your left ear, which was throwing off your balance.

That Monday in February at the cafe. You stand behind the counter, facing out the front window. It is bright outside, the kind that is not tricking you, the kind that is warm, heating sunlight. You can tell by the way people hold themselves—open, loose, demonstrative surface areas exposed, swaying, slowness. Casual, in the way that all people who grew up in California sunshine grow to be. Privileged by means of weather, not aristocratic bloodlines and old money.

You had gone to the shiny white burger place before the cafe. Sometimes you throw yourself into a glossy fast food joint, for the anonymity of it. You launch yourself through the doorway before you can change your mind, and once inside, you are grateful for the standardized booths and sanitation, glad that you won't see anyone you know there, or even want to know. Most likely, nobody will distract you, you won't be looking up every time the front door opens, because it will always be a disgruntled mother with crust-nosed children and a monstrous stroller struggling inwards.

You shut down, for a while, the expectation of sensory experiences. Nothing here is aesthetically pleasing. Nothing is charming, there is no character. The food tastes like nothing, like a processed capsule in the shape of food, with a vaguely foodlike soft texture, and that's it.

Later that afternoon at the cafe, you look outside, and after so many minutes, and so many people, a man walks jauntily by, facing you, and he looks happy, and your eyes catch, temporarily hook, and so you smile into the sun. He smiles back, and continues on his way, and then stops and turns back around and walks into the cafe. Hi, he says, and hi, you say back.

He tells you his name is Wade. You know him, from your friend Beatrice's photographs.

Within an hour of talking, he is telling you all the best secrets:

Hey, Banana. Here's How To Be More Like a Guy:

- Take what is offered to you
- Ask for what is not offered to you
- Be less nostalgic
- Don't think about/analyze love, relationships, sex

Within an hour of talking, you are telling him to get over himself a lot. This is because, you suspect, you are Chinese, and have ingrained in you, the bloody ways of humility. Modesty. Self-deprecation, in a not-joking kind of way. You are nothing, this is what you have been taught, what has been taught into you. Do not tempt the gods, the fates, destiny. Deny self-importance. Laugh at yourself. Stop taking yourself so seriously. Can you hear yourself? *Can you hear yourself.* If you can, you probably need to stop talking.

Hey, Banana. What is that, on your necklace, a machete?

What is that on your face, your mom?

I like that, your laugh.

Really? You laugh as you say this, even though you don't know why.

I like it. There's nothing like shy, unfettered laughter. It's sweet, it's unexpected.

Oh. Thanks I guess.

Slippery slope.

From laughter to what? you ask.

Love? At least a crush, for sure.

I like that you said sweet, you tell him, leaning in. I think that's a slippery slope.

Oh yeah? To what.

To terms of endearment. Honey. Sweetie. Baby. Sugar. Sweetiepie. Sweetheart. Sweetpea. Sunshine. Buttercup. Doll.

Dollface?

Not unless you're a mobster's gun moll girlfriend, you say very seriously. Um.

Kitten? Pussycat? Pussyface? Sweetcheeks? Chickadee? Bluebird? Sugarlips? Sodapop? Jellybean? Sugarcube? Ice cube? Saltwater taffy? Jawbreaker?

Marshmallow? Funnelcake? Cupcake? Ganache? Candy cane? Crumb cake? Fruit tart? Frangipane? Gumdrop? Gummy peach ring? Swedish fish? Turbinado sugar? You feel as if you could sit there for quite a while, swapping these words with him, exchanging them like candies.

For a while, each time after spending time with him, you silently repeat to yourself, take it easy, dollface.

&

I invent jealousy, and admiration, and alienation, between old friends, between two girls. But of course, these are not really things solely of my invention. Where imagination falters, perhaps I borrow generously from my own memories. Sometimes, I think there's not so much of a difference.

You're friends with a girl named Beatrice, an old-fashioned name for especially this girl, once you really got to know her. To you she seemed so cut-out-of-a-modern-cloth, a real contemporary doll, fast and bright and creative, forward-thinking, able to be so many things.

You, you are nothing. You float, are bodiless. You are a Chinese box. In sixth grade, you and Beatrice did a report on Guatemala, the quetzal that was the currency but also the huge multi-hued long-tailed bird. You did a gigantic replica of a Hershey's milk chocolate bar for a math proportions and ratios project. You also wrote about jellyfish—your father liked that. This turned out to be a seminal project for you, as years later, you still find yourself thinking about these lovely brainless floaty creatures.

Beatrice's family is from someplace on the East Coast like Stamford, Connecticut. So maybe the old-fashioned name did fit after all. You didn't know, though, you hadn't known people like that, what places like that meant, until you went to visit one summer.

You had no idea that there was a real culture of things like Nantucket reds and seersucker and whites between Memorial Day and Labor Day and L.L.Bean and names like Tibby and Tilly and Nelson and Bunny and Ted and summer homes and lake houses and Upstate and the Catskills and the Berkshires and the Cape and pants and belts with little embroidered animals on them, and deck shoes and boat shoes and duck shoes and whatever those other shoes were called and well, belts in general, people in California did not go around wearing belts all the time, and Martha's Vineyard and money. Where there were Juniors and III's, and ancestry could be traced, and things like names mattered. Out west, you didn't even have real names, your names were flip little things, pulled from the air, from the label on a refrigerator, from a movie star princess, from a transliteration or romanization of another language to English.

Summer is a verb there. As are school, and prep. People are slender and capable—that is the desired veneer: slender and capable. A murmur of correct words. Slender throats swallowing well-placed manners, words like wristwatches.

You, you have always had trouble with that. You are telling this story—you pretend to be a storyteller—but it is constant agony, each erratic word that falls out is another peck at your exposed liver by a giant eagle while you dangle from some cliff's precipice, stuck to a rock. You have no idea what these words must sound like to everyone else, if there even is any sound.

You rely on mythology, because without it, you search inside your head for words, and see only a big dark grotto.

Beatrice always said you were more querulous than garrulous.

Beatrice is the ultimate in slender and capable. Equestrian vocabulary seems to come to mind when you think of her, like breeding and carriage and comportment and poise, but they really are fitting. She has a younger sister, surely also slender and capable, whom you imagine wearing expensive gold bracelets on her thin wrists.

Bananas are like tampons, Beatrice is saying. She says things like that. She says things, to which you respond, who says that! Well, she does. Beatrice Lee says Things Like That. Bananas are like tampons, she is saying.

Necessary evils. Phallic and filling in a mercenary kind of way, a practical way to stuff it, but ultimately unpleasant and unsatisfying.

Beatrice is able to talk about bananas and tampons and still be classy about it, you don't know how. You think it might be this: she has the prettiest eyes and mouth. Steady and ethereal and soft. She might be talking about stuffing her face with penis or banana, which one nobody even knows, but she is so damn poised about it, you don't dare question how her elegance thrives even in vulgarity.

&

There is one scene from that summer when Beatrice and I were packing for the Europe trip, in our respective rooms, respective doors open. I was packing as if that summer I would be presented with the opportunity to impress all the boys in my life I had ever loved and lost. I looked down at the piles of clothing on my bed.

It was a joke. I ended up spending that summer sleeping with two married men. I was twenty-seven, and heartbroken, and my ripped flesh incanted to me that all was fair in love and war. That summer I felt wild and beautiful, I loved my body and the way it felt, the way it seemed to be working, how my skin was as glossy and smooth as glass, my limbs brown and flawless, my new hair choppy and free, swinging around my chin at will. I was with Beatrice, and I felt, from those men, that I was being looked at for the first time the way I had always seen men look at Beatrice. The way they would photograph her, spontaneously, as if they couldn't help it. As if even though they were professional photographers, they had never in their lives been so inspired to capture into stillness, to give permanence.

Beatrice knew it was a joke, my behavior a flourishment of bad ideas. I knew. I knew I had spent the first part of my twenties fucking up, and the next part of my twenties repenting and paying my dues in the form of loneliness. And now what? Spend all my life longing after people who already had someone else?

There is the fact that Helen is married:

You listed it as one of his flaws, even before you got married: not knowing when to stop. He admitted it. Wanting to push people, wanting to take things to the very edge, see how far he can go.

Well. This is where he could go, and then here is the other side of that.

You are cool, all right. You are cool, until you are not, cool, until you can't be cool, at which point you will remove yourself. You will extricate yourself before any kind of temper surfaces.

And now, you think, realize, that all your actions in life are attempts at connecting to other people. You are trapped in your separate bodies, you try to connect, through sex, through conversation, through seeing and listening, through telling stories, through family meals, and arguments, and traveling together, and saving each other, and resuscitating each other, and fighting each other, to merge, in some way, with other people. But how can you fight, how hard do you have to fight, to fight your way into someone else's body?

When I imagine Helen, she is always at home, alone in Los Angeles:

Turn on the water. Turn it on. There is no stopping it. There are forces, like gravity, and pressure. It is neverending; it streams, is streaming look at it go. Place the three middle fingers of your right hand under the water, palm side up, just the pads of your fingers under the water. You almost don't feel it. Wetness. What is that. It is nothing to you, you are not porous, it runs over you, you are a duck's back. Impermeable. Run-over.

Scissor-kick into the smooth piles of sheets on your bed. Nothing touches anything else, everything is tangled, your legs do not find each other. What does it matter, your legs do not feel all the way up, they end at the hips, they do not know, they only know that the rest of you breaks because they are kept prone, in your bed, while you sleep for a purpose, while you sleep certain feelings, certain consciousness away. You sleep things away, you kick things away, you push, and your legs move and wallow of their own accord, blind under the cover of your smooth, cool sheets.

It is possible to imagine another life, one that does not require depth of water, opaque mucous green of seaweed, tender green undersides of young herb leaves in the sun.

There is a knock, sharp, an ellipsis of rap rap rap that punctures these still photos. When someone shows up at your door, you have a choice to make. You don't sit up immediately, but the person inside of you sits up, alert. You send this inside person through the kitchen and living room to your front door. Refractory light bends its way around the corners of the front room, searching for a way in, out, hitting at fun-house mirror angles, trapped, an accidental leaf, twittery featherlight bird, juicy black fly, caught in a man-made box. You put yourself in boxes to stay organized, to keep track. You label each box, with the feelings meant for that box, with what is appropriate, keeping in mind phrases like *for someone of your station.* Sometimes, but rarely, you allow yourself to coat your body in slick black mascara, a thick oily layer on each and every lash. Lashes, lashes, lashing lashing lashing. Sometimes, you will spend a *significant chunk of time* trying on your fanciest dresses, which are kept crumpled and crying, folding in on themselves, fetal position, in the darkest wood-chipped corners of your dresser. You put on high heels, lifting one foot up and behind you at a time so that you can reach behind and slide the shoe on. You learned how to walk in heels when you turned eighteen. You met Wade that year.

Before, you had been afraid of what it might mean, if you cared about how you looked, if you brushed your hair, if you had a spread of lotions and perfumes and creams, piles of jewelry. You were afraid of leaving lipstick prints on glasses, of getting it on your teeth, of needing to touch up in a mirror or go to the bathroom every hour, of leaving a trail of foundation on sweaters and sheets. You were afraid of the morning someone might wake up next to you and be horrified of what you looked like with nothing on your face but yourself. You told him all these things, because he wanted to know. He made you agree with him on the state of your own beauty. The fact of it.

You look at your face in the bathroom mirror, a medicine cabinet triptych. Before, during, after. During, during, during. Now now now. Enduring. Endearing. Deer in headlights. You don't let yourself think about one thing, one word, for too long. Otherwise, you might tear your face off.

In this tripartite mirror, you try to see yourself as he might see you. You know he sees a different you, and you look for the different you in the warm moist air of the bathroom. You remind yourself that you give yourself, reasonably, you think, an *at-least-okay* in some pretty important departments: looks, smarts, humor, kindness. Isn't that enough, isn't that a lot? Isn't that good for someone? You look for the different you, you try to imagine someone who is all those things, probably, but also distinctly acerbic, sharp, sullen, blunt, silent, condescending, judgmental, intolerant, lazy, flaky, fickle, lost, hurt. You see that these things shine through all the holes, each one pricking a blinding bright point of light into his eyes, like the punctuation of a pin shooting through a single sheet of paper.

While you are in the bathroom, the knocking has stopped and started up again. You open the bathroom door. You walk across the kitchen floor. You place your hand on the cold round doorknob. You feel nothing, except for that. You know who it is. You know what you look like, to him. You can see yourself, framed in the doorway, impassive stare, the impasse is a truly unique confluence of expectation and hopelessness. Your hair in waves lets on nothing. Your black sweater says you are operating on the level of functionality. Certain things will function, like sleep, but there are ulterior motives, and he will see that. He will see you have been sleeping to get away.

When your husband shows up at your door, you have a choice to make.

You were not the type of girl one married. You thought you had made sure of that. Or, you were the type of girl who got married at nineteen. You are not so sure.

You open the door.

Hi, you say. You smile then. You are not supposed to, but seeing him makes you happy, and that feels simple, and you will take simplicity when it is offered like that.

What is not simple is the relief you feel, not in your head, but your body. You are able to change relief to antagonism if it is in your head, transform it into something more useful, something that shields, but with your body, you know less how to control.

There is the closing scene, a dinner, when I finally met her:

Last night, things turned. I guess, to put it concisely, succinctly, it was her turn. Dinner happened. I can describe it, but I don't even want to, it feels too brightly like wet paint, an open still-pulsing wound, blood is still coming out, turning things red. It's a pity. It's a shame. It's all of those things, that are petty and small, that I will turn petty and small, to belittle them, to deny them importance. Let's just say it was like watching the slaughter of a caged animal, from far away. Let's just say, I was getting farther and farther away, whether it was they who were receding, or I who was receding.

We sat at the square table, one person at each side. All squares are equilaterals but not all equilaterals are squares. All squares are rectangles but not all rectangles are squares. There was some sort of pithy logic to it, that always to me felt like fighting through hanging vines for a clearing, pulling apart interlocking strands of greenery, ripping apart grasping tendrils, rupturing ties. Just to get to what, to where.

Before, I hadn't noticed, hadn't predicted losing, because the walls of the enclosure were so far away, and far apart. They weren't even touching each other. There were no vertices, no corners, only four straight lines.

I didn't notice their approach. My sister will betray my trust like that, without even calling it betrayal. This is *life*, she insists.

And now, we sat at the square table, and Helen's voice was not low and scrapey and wise like I imagined, but poured forth words like cream, like polished crystal gems, each sentence baubling against the last and next like the sound of sophisticated glass.

Let's just say, I wanted to shoot myself, repeatedly. Let's just say, sure, tell me the story of your lives, and the story of your love, and, well, don't expect me to not shoot myself, repeatedly.

What was the worst, was her laugh. In my imaginings, I had allowed her to laugh, but I hadn't made predictions about it, I hadn't imagined it with the sound on.

R

She was always at home, alone. Me, too, though; I am also at home, alone:

I open the door from my bedroom to the kitchen. The air in the rest of the apartment is cooler, faster, it moves as if there is life, as if it is filled with plants, transpiring, respiring, breathing in and out, in and out, chlorophyll pulsating in veins, pumping oxygen into the atmosphere. The kitchen and living room are dim, the curtains on the far side of the wall behind the couches sway silently.

The kitchen counter around the sink is cluttered with wares of all types, clattered against each other in a still life. Balanced plates, mugs, saucers, spoons, glass plates stacked unevenly. There is a bag of bread sitting diagonally, cross-sectioning the bottom left corner of the sink. There is a ghost white cutting board, on which lies one red bell pepper.

The bell pepper is helpless on its side. Several slivers have already been gouged from it. These red strips are piled neatly toward the top left of the cutting board, like logs.

My mother used to comment on my reticence, would remark that I held onto my words as if they were gold. Which seemed to be less a comment on material greed than on my general unwillingness to let go of something thought of as a precious commodity.

I have become very good at not saying anything, for prolonged periods of time.

All of my heroes have been leavers.

But I see that the rest of the bell pepper lolls there, balanced on the fulcrum of a rounded edge. The dim morning light glosses a slight creamy sheen on one bulbous side surface. It flounders, wonders where the rest of its body has gone. I'm on fire, the pepper whispers, quietly. A six-inch valley has been cut, the hissing of skin and flesh being sliced in one long, whispering motion.

So I step quietly across the warm stone floors toward the pepper. The tiles feel soft, in this silence and heat. If the room is turning into a forest, I think I may be slowly sinking with each step, down, into the fecund black soil of the forest floor, a loosely moist filling of roots and leaves, detritus and insect bodies, wings and feet and stick-like ribbed abdomens.

In the light of morning, I wake up and turn onto my side. I raise my right arm into the air of the forest, wiggle my fingers, flex them open. My hand feels slightly numb. My right jaw aches, and turning my wrist, I see the rich teeming brown of the soft soil beneath me.

It sounds like nothing. *It sounds like nothing.* It *is* nothing.

I see a red mark on my forearm, not a cut, nothing breaking through skin, but a long red mark, and a small bruise-colored mark below it, like an exclamation point. ! Yes. ! You did it! Go! Wow!

Sometimes, my heart beats faster, and I don't want it to. Sometimes, I think, I'm trying, I'm trying to grow, and be a better person, and progress, and evolve, and figure things out, and fix things that I've broken along the way.

I pull my eyelids down, for a moment, like a test. Can you do it. Do this. Do this, at this speed. I continue to rotate my wrist, hand up in the air. Cracking. Sometimes my arms are made of knives, sometimes of feathers. I warm them up, until there is no more cracking. Only the faintest high-pitched flit of a solid surface cutting through the air.

Ghosts

Ghost #1

WE CALLED HER the Early Twenties Girl Ghost. She was in her early twenties, not from the 1920s. I was working late alone in the lofted office. The back door of the building clicked metallically open and closed, and a few seconds later, through the spaces between the beams of the guardrail, I saw her walk the length of the northern half of the downstairs space from where I sat. I saw her from the back. I had not yelled out hello when the door first opened, and I could not yell hello now. She disappeared into the corridor that led to the storefront, which was locked up for the night. I sat for a moment longer, my hands paralyzed in home row position over my keyboard. I clenched my teeth experimentally. I rolled my eyeballs around in their sockets. I was resolving, or was I dissolving. I stepped carefully across the office, and went downstairs. I retraced her steps. I was following the footsteps of a ghost and I didn't even know it. Or I knew it, but didn't want to admit it. I went through the corridor. I pushed aside the plastic curtain. Hello, I finally ventured. But she was a ghost. There was no body to be found.

Ghost #2

We called it the Phantom of the Bathroom. The restaurant had just closed, the final diners had just left. We were doing closing work. I went to check on the bathroom, a one-room ordeal in the back near the ice machine. There was a Chinese restaurant we used to go to a lot, called Pavilions. It was shaped like a pagoda, like a huge fat white pagoda like a big block of tofu. The bathroom in Pavilions was in the back, down a corridor. In one corner near the entrance of the corridor was a vending machine selling cigarettes. I liked looking at the buttons, each button had on it a different miniature image of a carton of cigarettes. I liked miniature things. I liked the idea of things getting smaller and smaller, but not disappearing.

This Chinese restaurant was not like Pavilions. But someday I would be remembering it. I did not like to think of that, because you only remember things if they've gone away. Or if you yourself have gone away.

This Chinese restaurant had a smooth brass peacock-shaped coat hook on the back of the bathroom door that I coveted. I looked at it whenever I was in the bathroom. I was planning on looking at it then, when I was checking on the bathroom. I turned the doorknob, but it wouldn't turn, because it was locked. I turned it again. I knocked. Hello? I said. I did not hesitate to say hello then, I was racing to finish my closing work. Is anyone there, I said to the door, knocking on it again. I went to go find Candy who was reconciling receipts behind the bar at the front of the restaurant. Everyone is gone, right? I asked. She nodded. No, I said. But the bathroom's locked. I don't know if someone is in there. I mean, I think maybe there's nobody in there. I think maybe it got accidentally locked from the inside. That's what I said, even though it doesn't make sense. It was locked from the outside, with nobody inside, accidentally. She shrugged. She was worried about failing her Italian class, because then she wouldn't be able to do her summer study abroad in Milan. I went to look for Jake. Hey, the bathroom's locked from the inside, I said. Do you know where the key is, how do we get it open? There's a key in the desk downstairs in the office, he said. But the office door is locked and Bo is the only one with the key and he just left. Ugh, I said. I went to go find a knife in the drawer by the tea station. I wiggled the tip of the knife around in the keyhole in the middle of the doorknob. I jiggled the doorknob at the same time, with my left hand. It still wouldn't open. Jake, I called over my shoulder. I jiggled the knife again, and then the doorknob turned, and I pushed open the door but it immediately hit—softly but forcefully—someone right inside the door OH I exclaimed as the door slammed shut again OH shit sorry I didn't mean—, I exclaimed in shock. Jake arrived then. What are you doing, he said rolling his eyes. I was shaking. From what I'm not sure. No, no, there's someone in there, there IS someone in there, I said. I didn't know what I was saying, but there you go. Jake reached over and turned the doorknob and opened the door. But there was nobody inside. I felt it, I felt the door hit a body, I was telling Candy up at the front. She turned on the soundtrack from The Phantom of the Opera then, the music swelling up to fill every possible space.

Ghost #3

I thought of her as the Hotel Water Tower Ghost. I watched as she walked into the hotel. I watched as she stopped at the front counter, and then followed as she paused by the elevators, and then seemingly changed her mind, and walked up the stairs instead. Once inside her room, she seemed lost, unsure of what to do, or what she should be doing, or perhaps unsure of something she had already decided, something she had already put into motion. She walked around the room for a while, looking at things, touching things, picking things up and putting them back down. She ate a sandwich outside, she looked up at the building, at the sky, even up at the roof, it seems. I imagine that her gaze lingered on the roof, but perhaps I project that lingering in hindsight, knowing that the roof would be where her body ended. She went back into her room, and she sat down on the bed and wrote in her notebook for a while. I watched her as she wrote. I read over her shoulder. Unremarkable observations, perhaps belying some deeper guilt or fear, something darker. She didn't seem to be in the right place, there in that hotel, with her glasses and her ponytail, her hooded college sweatshirt and jeans, her backpack. A lot of people in that hotel are lonely, but she, she didn't seem to be in the right place.

I have never been in a hotel like this before. There was nobody at the front desk when I walked through the entrance last night. A bell hanging from a string on the door. There was something muffled about my room. I put my backpack down on the chair next to the window. Outside, it was dark, a few people walked on the street below—they looked slow, and aimless, like they had nowhere important to be. The high wail of sirens coming closer and then getting farther away. I unzipped my backback and pulled my sandwich out. After the siren, the room became very quiet. Every sound I heard was smooth like bubbles. Voices from people, or from a TV, or a radio. Space sounds, buzzing, or humming, from machinery. I turned on the bathroom light. I turned it off. I picked up my room key from the nightstand, and walked out to the balcony that wrapped around the building. I ate my sandwich while I leaned against the railing. I thought about calling Mom. I thought about calling someone. Just so I could hear someone familiar talking, and then hear the pause, and then hear my own voice responding. Talking about nothing. I looked up and down the hallway. Every room door was the same. All painted the same peach color. I pressed my fingers against the sharp bumps of the stucco wall. Leaning back against the railing, I looked up at the next floor of rooms. Rows and rows of shut doors. I could not imagine what might be happening behind those closed doors. At some point, I think, there are too many possibilities, for what people could be doing. There was a metal ladder at the far end of the building, for access onto the roof. I could see the edges of things that were on the roof, walled-off rectangular structures, a utility room, something with engines, turbines, water, wires, electricity.

"The notebook that was found among the victim's belongings was blank except for the first four pages. The first page contained a list of names and phone numbers, all confirmed to be members of the victim's immediate family, friends, or classmates. The other three pages have the appearance of handwritten diary entries, and are dated the night of the homicide. These entries consist predominantly of the victim's observations of the hotel, and record her actions upon entering the room, and then as she exits the room to the exterior balcony. Apart from the recollection of a childhood memory in another hotel, the contents of the notebook provide little insight into the victim's background, and give no concrete indication of her intentions for the night, nor any knowledge or foresight of an encounter with the perpetrator."

Ghost #4

I called him the Ghost Dude. He wasn't dead, and he wasn't invisible, but he was very pale, and he always looked like he was doing some serious soul-searching when he looked at me while we were having sex. I wasn't sure what he was planning on doing, if he should really end up finding my soul or his own soul in the depths of my face while his penis was heaving itself in and out of my vagina. But I was sure that I didn't have it in me, to allow it to happen, so I closed my eyes, or I leaned over or turned around or stuffed my face into the bed or a pillow. Look at me, he would say, and I would do the opposite. I looked out the window, there was a field outside that window by his bed, which later, after when we weren't having sex anymore, a bunch of us would be playing bocce ball in that field, and I would get hundreds of mosquito bites, which had never been a concern for me at all, and from that point onward, I would always get hundreds of mosquito bites, wherever I went. Once, we had sex on his wool couch while *Over the Top*, that Sylvester Stallone arm-wrestling movie, played on his huge screen. I had wished for his body to be invisible, so that I could watch the movie. Don't you want to touch me, he had asked me the first time we had sex, because I had let him touch me, but somehow could not find it within me the desire to touch him back. With some people, you win, every point of contact is a fucking wonder, you have never loved such skin, such flesh. With the Ghost Dude, I closed my eyes and still I saw his eyes, wide and guileless, probing into mine. What do you call someone who makes you want to become invisible? It was possible, I knew, because it had happened to me once before, with some people, to feel as if each time you were looked at, you yourself had become a new way of seeing. Would you like to be made and remade each time someone looked at you?

I did, once. Before I ever saw any ghosts.

But back to Ghost Dude. His eyes searched in mine, as if he were a ghost looking for a host body to inhabit. Longing. I shied. I had found him, in my community college Spanish class, which I was taking for professional development. He was the sous chef at a local restaurant, and was trying to supplement his kitchen Spanish with some textbook basics. He looked for me, even as he looked at me. I got a rug burn from having sex on his wool couch. He was from North Dakota, where perhaps wool couches made sense; here in L.A., I dreamed of destroying that wool couch, with a medieval axe.

Ghost #5

It didn't take so long to become a Secret Ghost. I canceled on everything. I stopped responding. I didn't make a sound. Not a wind. There was no sheerness, no faint outline. Not even a wisp. Even back when I was solid and stubbornly obstructive, I used to sit very still sometimes, in moments of pain. I could picture in vivid glistening blood red, the ripping out of my heart, after each one of my three heartbreaks, like in that movie when the possessed boy-king sticks his hand straight into that guy's chest and pulls out a fistful of still-beating pulp, handful of heart. I was used to responding to emotional havoc by staying perfectly motionless, breath illegible.

I think it first began with Omar when we ended up sharing a cab back to Costa Mesa after the pastry chef's wedding. We were both holding glass cylinders bursting up and out with flowers and fronds. The centerpieces had not looked so big on the tables at the reception, but now, in the cab, the flora seemed to engulf the entire backseat. I had poured out some of the water from mine, but he had not poured any out of his, and now these aggressive life forms were precariously balanced on our respective laps as the car careened through the streets. My skirt was riding up, and I pulled it down. He glanced down at me as I adjusted the skirt, and then looked back out the window on his side. When I think about this cab ride later on, I mostly remember a moment when I semi-drunkenly and mock-indignantly asked loudly into his face, what you don't *trust* me?! and though I don't recall what words led up to this or what words came after, I do distinctly recall his expression of bemusement, and my feeling that his failure to immediately cede ground was some sort of challenge.

Our first hangout after I quit the restaurant, I met Omar at The Quiet Woman, a bar on PCH in Corona del Mar. What am I doing here, I had laughed when I found him at the bar, already mid-drink. I pawed the area beneath the counter, feeling for a hook, and finally bent over to peer into the darkness.

He shrugged and smiled wide at me. Just hanging out, he said. It was one a.m. I had quit the restaurant four months ago. He'd already had two whiskeys. He bought me a drink, then another. We argued over who was paying. There was a lot of pushing back and forth of credit cards, but it was creating a scene, so I stopped. I owe you, come on, he said. What? What do you owe me for, I asked. You'll see, he said. I laughed and snorted so hard whiskey sputtered out both my nose and my mouth, sting tearing through my entire nasal cavity, my eyes burning. The sunblock and sweat on my eyelids must have been melting into my eyes.

We moved to one of the booths in the back. We sat next to each other in the booth. I swallowed. I breathed in and out. I could tell that he was looking at me. We were sitting next to each other, but not touching, but as close as it's possible to be next to another person without touching. It's possible to be very close and still not touch. He leaned in. I sat stock-still. Possums do this. Other animals do this. Play dead. Deer in headlights. Possums get run over all the time. Once, in my parents' backyard, they found a dead possum, but it was really dead. But inside it, were babies that were alive. Animal control came and picked all of them up, they reassured me that the babies would be okay.

Why would they be okay? Why would a life of resorting to playing dead be okay? Still I did not move. I could feel his breath on my left ear and cheek. He started to say something, but stopped, and instead moved his mouth to behind my ear. Still I think, we were not touching. But I could feel his breath and now, the humidity of his breath. Warm. A cloud misted just inside the entrance of my vagina. It was creating its own cloud. Cumulus-pulse. When a cloud gets too heavy, it must dispel all its liquid. I squeeze my legs closer together. My hands are clenched together, in a prayer position, squeezed into the space between my thighs. Keep it the fuck together, I think to myself. The tip of his tongue, is touching me now, just behind my ear lobe. One of his hands is at the nape of my neck, a firm clarifying massage. The other hand is lightly running up my bare arm. I feel his breath and the tongue, relaxed, slowly licking at my neck. His nose is pressed into the edge of my hairline. He inhales.

After Omar ended, I couldn't help feeling that I'd had my heart fucked over. I wondered if I'd ever feel as seen, as understood, as resonant, with another person as I did with Omar. This is a classic, time-tested feeling—it's basically the premise of all rom-coms and rom-drams. The certainty that in this lifetime, I will only ever have that one window of time, one spring and summer in my life, to be perfectly clear, and all other times before and after I will only be a blur, hazy, half out the door. Nobody would be able to see me. Not all of me. Only a leg here, a profile there. A swatch of skin.

On the phone, my mother brings up again the Chinese boy who was forced at gunpoint to drive the Boston marathon terrorist bombers around for a while. My mother is obsessed with the fact that the boy's roommate was worried that he hadn't come home. See, she says, it's really good to have someone like that. I worry about you. You don't have a boyfriend or husband. Back when you lived with your friend, she would notice if you didn't come home one night, right? Right, I think, but Holly also betrayed me in a love triangle situation you know nothing about and now we are barely even friends anymore. I just worry, she continues. That you don't have that now. What would happen? Would your coworkers notice? Do you have neighbors or friends or people who would notice if you disappeared? How long would it take for people to notice that you're gone? Well, I say to my mother, *you* would notice. I am unable to peel away a thick nasty feeling as I say this.

While becoming a ghost, you begin to understand what it's like to almost feel nothing—if you're in just the right place, the right position, and stayed perfectly still. No breeze over the skin from moving through time and space. Just a river slipping by before your eyes that doesn't even really register. Background, wallpaper.

Now that I am no longer solid, now that I am slippery and borderless, if I stay still like that, I become a secret. Perhaps only one person ever invented me, and I've been forgotten. Perhaps I never was there at all, and am not there now. I shift, in overlapping circle motions, to pay a ghastly visit to Holly. Or Omar. Same thing now. Holly was the former roommate, my flighty friend, full of blonde hair and squawky ideas. Holly's ideas leapt out of her fully formed, like Athena out of Zeus's head. She animated them into being, and people gawked, were flabbergasted, blown away, they bought into it hook, line, and sinker. She opened her eyes wide and fluttered her dark lashes and chewed on her own lips while she presented her incisive mind to the world, and we all prostrated ourselves before her feet. She wore all the time those black cloth Mary Jane slippers, she would wear them down, and then go buy another pair in Chinatown for five bucks.

Holly wasn't home, but most likely Omar was home, and so I slipped through room after room until I found him in the back of the house. He was arranging pieces of paper on a big table, they looked like poems, one poem per sheet. As the Secret Ghost, I couldn't really see very well from a distance. Anyone could see right through me, but my own senses had been fogged up, and my memory too. I could barely make out the words two feet away.

I stood next to Omar. I tested my inconsequentiality, overlapping with him a little and then a lot. I felt nothing. But this was a good thing. I try to touch my mouth to his neck, to press my body lightly against his. But there is only air. I tell myself this is okay too. This new me, this Secret Ghost me, has no ability—and subsequently, no need—for old modes of contact: squeezing and clenching, pushing and pressing, pulling and skimming, grasping and clutching. There was no need to keep it the fuck together, there was nothing to keep together, everything was apart, like the coldly distant light of stars pricking a dark sky, all separate, all from a different time, all out of arm's reach.

A Golden State

GIVEN THE OPTION, I will stand at the kitchen counter, in the late afternoon, in April, or September, and eat marinated artichoke hearts out of the can, while staring out the kitchen window, for all time. Given the option, I will stare until I become a statue, the seasons passing in the reflections of my eyes, and no other movement.

At the moment, I was staring out the window of my parents' car. As a kid, I had clocked thousands of hours staring out very similar backseat windows on family road trips to San Diego, to Sequoia, to Yellowstone, to Lake Tahoe, to Mammoth, to Lake Arrowhead, Big Bear, Cedar Lake. Even a drive to the San Gabriel Valley felt like a road trip then. Picture this: an ivory-colored station wagon. The mother with a plastic sun visor on her head, permed hair, glitter puffy paint in a smattering of decorative daubs on the top of the visor. The father, also with a sun visor, but his is cloth, with a terrycloth interior, and an anchor or golfing logo or insignia of some kind on the top. In the backseat, one sister a teenager. That is enough, that is everything about that sister, at this moment in time. The other, younger sister, sits on the other side of the backseat. She faces out the window at her side, eyes skimming barely, lightly, just on the surface of the passing hillsides, the gray blur of highway asphalt and fences, orange and almond tree groves. The occasional bright silver fluttering of reflective mylar ribbons, keeping the birds away.

Twenty years later. I might as well be in that same car, isolated backseat statuette, staring out the window, friendly only with the flat hills, the flat line of the sky, the unseeing, impenetrable cerulean blue of the sky. The sky that gave nothing of itself. Thousands of hours spent watching, sullenly, angst-ridden, not speaking, the pale peach and white stucco buildings streak by, the tans, and dusty greens, and sandy browns, the sharp skinny angles of palm trees, the patches of wild sagebrush. Thousands of hours passively absorbing the rows and rows of orange and almond tree groves—they would appear like just another random swath of trees, and then a magical moment: click, shift, at the right second, the one moment as the car aligned, and you saw that it wasn't a random scattering at all, they were all in perfectly straight rows, line, after line, after line.

The city of Irvine had only been around for ten years when my parents moved there; it was just now celebrating its thirty-fifth birthday. It was the paradigm of sterile, new, clean, safe, planned suburb: sprawling California ranch homes, California schools (outdoor picnic benches instead of an indoor cafeteria?! Blew people's minds! You *always* ate outside? Yes. What if it's cold? It's not ever. What if it rains? It doesn't ever.) set against a landscape that still had a bit of a feel of the frontier, still held seemingly infinite expanses of chaparral hills, tumbleweeds, golden poppies, coyotes, quails, and roadrunners. Hawks perched on lamp posts. Mostly I remember liking being out in our mild southern California nature. It was a break from my sister, from my completely uncomprehending parents, it was quiet and let me be quiet, it asked nothing of me. My grandfather had given my sister and me these National Geographic children's pop-up books one Christmas. I remember in particular, *Creatures of the Desert World*: rabbits, lizards, coyotes, rattlesnakes. It looked like my home, the same distinct color palette, the same rough textures.

The house my parents lived in now they had moved into after I finished high school, a house in Newport Ridge North, a gated community developed by the fine colorless folks at Pelican Hill Real Estate. A house, AKA a "luxury property." Newport Ridge North was Provençal-themed, meaning nobody could pronounce any of the street names (Fayence, Musset, Nerval, Seyne, Reiz, Bandol, Tarascon, Ferrand, Ronsard, Lemans, Vincennes, Jarden, Sommet), and you were given a list of trees you were allowed to plant in your front yard, and recommended groundcover and flowers and shrubs. You were fined if you (or, more realistically, your gardener) didn't keep your grass green and mowed, though in times of drought watering schedules were put into place. Every time I entered the community, the huge gold letters of Newport Ridge North set against a wall of stone slabs, the gatehouse where the security guard waved, the agonizing slowness of the clanking gate as it rolled open, I ogled the smooth spotless blackness of the asphalt inside this Newport Ridge North, so freshly black I always thought it had just been raining, when really, the homeowners' association fees must have been funneled into the very urgent task of constantly paving and repaving the streets.

The house I had grown up in was about fifteen minutes away, across the street from my elementary and middle schools: Bonita Canyon, and Rancho (mascot: the Conquistador!). The edge of the school grounds abutted Chaparral Park, which led into several miles of unpaved trails, and some hills of decent elevation, upon which we gathered to watch fireworks on the Fourth of July. From there, an open view of Orange County, the Santa Ana mountains, Catalina Island. About 500 meters south of my house lay the northern border of Bommer Canyon, 16,000 acres of, well, canyon. We did a lot of school projects focused on the American West: I built a miniature replica of Anasazi cliff dwellings out of brown paper grocery bags. I wrote extensive reports on ranching, Cochise, cattle-branding (we designed our own branding iron symbols), the California missions. We took field trips to Mission San Juan Capistrano and Knott's Berry Farm, a kind of western-wilderness-gold-mining-ghost-town type of theme park. We had extensive units on the Gold Rush, and various mining techniques.

At that house on Flintridge Street, I did my homework at the breakfast nook every afternoon. I would stare out the window. The curtains were white with an orange floral, vinelike motif at once bright and faded. I would watch the slight slant of the hills in the distance, almost always a beige-tan color, sometimes with a few scattered dark blips—"Oh, cows," my sister and I would say, and turn back to our homework.

Once, two decades earlier, flames came over the top of the hills we looked at from that breakfast nook. We could see from the upstairs windows, people on their roofs in the Sierras (what we called the group of homes sandwiched between Turtle Rock Drive and Bonita Canyon Drive, all the street names started with Sierra—Sierra Luna, Sierra Noche, Sierra Siena, Sierra Nuevo) hosing their roofs down, inky smoke rising up over the ridges. We evacuated in the evening, up toward the northern part of the city, packed my mother's ivory-colored diesel station wagon.

Up in the front of the car, my parents began arguing over the air conditioning. Right now, the car was making its way down Barranca, or Culver, where a new row of ready-made storefronts and restaurants had popped up like movie lot facades: top shops that form the generic nucleus of any city in the U.S.—California Pizza Kitchen, The Cheesecake Factory, K-Mart, Sprinkles, Whole Foods, Trader Joe's, Fleming's Steakhouse, Barnes & Noble, a flashing multi-shoppertainment-movieplex, Starbucks or Coffee Bean, Houston's.

I think back to New York. These days. These days, those past tense days. I hadn't known that in a new city, on a new coast, that my body would be different, would feel like somebody else's object, a horror movie alien.

In the winter, in the locker room in a ceramics studio in the Village, I was rolling up my shirtsleeves, and could not recognize the pale forearms that appeared. They were not mine. In the summer, in a used bookstore near Union Square, I saw a book that reminded me of the golden boy. I tilted the book out of the bookshelf. It wasn't too hard, to pull it out, the bookstore's foreign language poetry section was small, the books stood loosely. And yet, the book gave a crack when I flipped it open. A bug flew out, and towards my face. I jerked my head back, fingers brushing instinctively in front of my eyes. Had it flown into my eye, gotten caught in my eyelashes? This would be a fear of mine. I quickly slid the book back into its place on the shelf. It all depends on whether or not you choose to believe in omens. Whether or not you choose to assign meaning.

From the front of the car, my parents pointed out that we were on the Grapevine. They were referring to an incident from my past. Once, here, in the beating dry heat of late summer, I sat twisted around in the passenger side seat of my gold sedan, watching my boyfriend of seven months getting arrested through the dusty rear window. He was being slammed against the hood of the highway patrol car, he was being handcuffed. We were on the Grapevine, this very same stretch of it, in Bakersfield. We had been headed to Morro Bay for a short camping trip. The officers claimed to have clocked him with a radar gun going 120 miles per hour. I ended up spending a night camped out on a bench in the waiting room of the Kern County Jail, waiting for him to be released. The backseat and trunk of my gold car which was parked in the empty jail parking lot was full of camping food and whiskey. I sat there on the bench that night thinking about the beef jerky in the car. The parking lot was empty. Sand all around. Ghosts everywhere.

He had been from the Twin Cities. I wrote pages and pages of poetry about how much I despised the Midwest, even though my on-the-ground knowledge of it consisted solely of two days in Chicago. I wrote that I hated how they pronounced "bags" and how the cities looked, and how uncynical and white and happy and protected the people I had met were. I never told him any of that. I shared with him what I thought was somewhat harmless, things like how I could not wrap my head around what a casserole was or why meatloaf existed. Actually I didn't even say that second one, that might have been too aggressive, too leading. He was proud of his hometown; it's actually very diverse, he told me, we have the second biggest Hmong population there.

I smiled and said something unintelligible to my parents, something about how long ago it was, when that had all happened. I could say these generic phrases, all day long. I could talk about things that didn't matter, that weren't secrets, for all time. Here in the southland, I was more able to keep myself secret. Sometimes, during the day, I walked through the brush. I slipped my fingers into the chaparral, tips brushing the dry brittle tips, the tender thorns. The browns and brown greens coated my eyes, slicked them, licked them, affectionate tongues, rough and hot and damp. It suddenly felt like all my life I had been needing to get back to this, the gray browns, the tan browns, the sand browns, beige browns of sharp rocks scattered like hazards on sand. All these dry bits on one plane, a flat photograph of desiccation. But that was the trick. These things were alive. Their camouflaged lives soothed me in a way that the alien green abundance of the deciduous woods back around New York could not dare touch.

I had been living in a quasi-converted loft in Bushwick in those years. In the mornings, I would walk through the quiet living room space into the bathroom. The bathroom sink had been not draining well for at least half a year. There was a lot of gunk in there. A lot of saliva, and old rotting food bits, and mucous, and phlegm, and soap residue, and bits and pieces of hair, and dead skin flakes, and bugs, and it was all coagulated into a very dank, foul, almost edible stench. Gooily coating the pipes. Gooily accumulating, layer upon bumpy layer. As a result, there were tiny flies, gnats, that hovered around the openings of the sink. I would walk back to my bedroom.

I look back upon that time as if it were a long time ago, and I think to myself, ah, yes, those years in Bushwick. That had been the era of the golden boy. Before I met the golden boy, in New York, the kind of thing that would happen to me would be that I would be having an affair with some guy, and we would go get a hotel somewhere on some night. We would forget to eat dinner. I would try to give this guy a blow job and he would just turn out to be way too big, horrifyingly too much. I would just not finish, my eyes tearing, and slobber and sticky liquids everywhere. The sheets would have been hotel starched, and then they would have been soaked through. He would spank me, and the sting would float from my skin and hover in the air for a cool and glorious second. I would wait for the beat of silence, before I felt his hand. I would wait for that slappy sound. Even though he was just some guy, we might fall asleep curled together on the dry side of the bed, holding hands. And the next morning, we would go for a quick swim in the hotel pool, and the pool boy setting up poolside for the day would kind of look familiar and then I would realize with a dawning shock that he was one of my former interns.

I would wade and waver in the water, tilting my face away from him. I would swim five laps, hoping not to have a confrontation with the pool boy. I would hold my breath.

In my room early in the mornings, I would look in the mirror. There might be a bruise on my left butt cheek. Later, before heading out, I would poke a curious finger at another bruise, high up my leg at the inside of my thigh, prod the burgeoning bluing of pale, fatty flesh. I had to take two trains to work. My right knee had a bruise on it, and then I noticed a smaller one adjacent to the one in the center. By the second train, the two had combined to form one large purple reddish bruise, covering the entirety of my kneecap. I had on some cutoff denim shorts and waited for someone on the subway to notice my bruised knee, to ask what happened, so that I could say, oh, that's just from having sex on my knees. But nobody said a thing, if anyone was glancing at my legs, they were probably first noticing the mosquito bite scars on my shins. This was the kind of thing that would happen to me, in New York. Before the era of the golden boy.

The golden boy held me in his mouth. Hanging between slackened jaws, was it a holding position of protection or of hunger, appetite, consumption? I had a long neck. The drawing teacher at the community college in L.A. told me so, when I used to model for life drawing classes at night. I wore a wool miniskirt, and a button-down collared shirt with French cuffs. It's not really necessary to even own a wool skirt in Los Angeles, wool anything barely. There had been years in my life in the southland, when I had bought clothing for future, other selves. In preparation of a newly-emerged self, that was waiting somewhere on down the road. I couldn't ever catch up.

I was taking my time. I stretched my long neck to see over people's heads. I wanted all or nothing. Once, when I came home, the golden boy had hung my curtains up in my room. He had installed the curtain rod attachments, and placed the curtain rod in its place, and threaded the curtains onto the rod. The curtains billowed in like storybook sails. They were relentless. I called him to ask him about the curtains. I thought it would be a nice gesture, he said. I said thank you, and asked him what he thought about the word, gesture. Really, I was just trying to see if, like me, he saw something futile in the word gesture. Gestures were usually faint shadows of real things, the small thing you did, or showed, or gave, because you were unable to do, or show, or give, the actual, real, big, important thing. Instead of calling me ungrateful, which I had already done, to myself, in my head, he was quiet. Your roommate let me in, he said. Your roommate let *me* in—a strange man, with paint on his face, holding an electric drill. You're not a strange man, I said, and thought I would accompany this statement with a laugh, but found that in the saying of it, it had transformed in my head, from something humorous, to something sobering and painful.

We soon moved into a new apartment together. I would stand in the doorway of the bedroom which was right off the kitchen, watching him cook lunch, which would go into small glass containers that he settled into the bottom of his backpack. Other things in the backpack included a notebook, a book, pen, sometimes some articles of clothing or accessories, sometimes a power drill, or measuring tape, an extra pair of pants or long underwear, a six pack of cold beers. He might be cooking rice and beans, in a camping pot. He had gotten it in his head that for the sake of potential apocalypse, or just for camping, to build up a thorough camping equipment setup, for every new household item we needed, he would buy the camping version. Always be ready to live off of survival-mode-type accoutrements. Instead of a bed, why not buy a sleeping bag? Instead of a room, why not just have tents, I had asked, trying to be very precisely one-half funny, one-half error-of-your-ways serious. Very quickly, all of our kitchen equipment became the camping version of things. All of our lamps were hand-wound flashlights. We kept a tub of sand by the kitchen sink, and scrubbed our camping pots and pans and tin mugs with a handful of sand and a sponge.

Sex in a sleeping bag was still sex. Maybe it was even more—sex contained, in a bag. (We were like a ship in a bottle, the golden boy and me.

How did we get here, after that disaster of our first go-around the previous year? Impossible ship, in an impossible bottle.) Sometimes, when it was hot, on top of the sleeping bag. For two bodies to be helplessly, violently, thrusting and butting at each other, thwacking and clapping at each other. Hopeless urgency. I was obsessed with body parts of sense, touching body parts of sense. Mouth to ear. Nose to eye.

There in that apartment I shared with the golden boy, sometimes, watching him naked, in one of the tiny rooms, I was struck with a sense of wonder. We would be fighting over a towel, as per usual, because, as per usual, he would be trying to go take a shower using my still-damp towel, and I would be trying to get him to take a clean, or at least, dry towel. And I would be struck that this was somehow my life, that he was in it, that I had him for the moment. It was something, all right. Maybe the only thing.

When we moved in together, I'd had to tell my parents about him. What does he do? they asked. By then, the golden boy was in grad school at Teachers College up at Columbia. Did you know that Georgia O'Keeffe studied there? And Dr. Ruth? Wow, they marveled, impressed. Who is Dr. Ruth? they asked. What's he going to do after school? they asked. He's in the counseling and clinical psychology department, I said, instead of offering the more specific information that within that department, the golden boy was at the new Spirituality Mind Body Institute. He was studying ancient healing practices with a cohort of aspiring "mind-body healers" and "spiritual activists," promoting self-actualization and "inner work for outer change." So he's your boyfriend? my parents asked. If you're living together, that means he's really important to you, huh? I mean, I guess he's a pretty important part of my life, I said.

I could not bring myself to say that he was important to me directly. His body to my body. The best I could do was say he was a pretty important part of my life, as if my life was an object separate from me, something that had maybe just fallen out of my pocket, something that could just be lying around. What is his family like, they asked. I was silent. Where is he from? they asked. Nebraska, I said. Is he white? they asked. Mm hmm, I said. What was he doing before school? they asked. He was an art handler, and he also had his own company, I said, he and his best friend from college started up a nonprofit kombucha brand that got pretty big, I said. They sell it everywhere, they sell it at Whole Foods. He sounds great, my parents said. Even better than the other ones before, they said. You know, we always liked a lot of those guys from before. You were always with good guys. They're all married now, but they could have married you. You know, you should make sure he knows that you're serious. You want to start a family, you're getting older. What is your five-year plan?

I don't say anything. I stare straight ahead at the blank white wall, waiting for something to appear. I want to scream at them. I want to say, that I'm serious? Am I serious? Do you want me to be serious the way you guys were serious? So serious that you remain in a marriage that for so many years has just been wearing you down, destroying you quietly, shrinking your hearts to nothing?

My parents are playing Simon & Garfunkel. I pretend to be asleep. It is quiet up in the front of the car, aside from the low-volume music. My dad is driving, my mom is staring straight ahead. There is a distinct column of empty space between them; both of their forearms are resting on the center console, but not touching. Squinting does not bring them any closer to touching. I have a distinct memory of being on airplanes, as a kid, on family vacations, and my mom insisting we sleep, or even if we couldn't fall asleep, just rest, and pretend to sleep. I would close my eyes while she was turned around in her seat in front of me, making sure that my eyes were closed, and then once she turned back around, I would open my eyes the slightest crack, and try to watch the movie that was playing on the big screen in the front. Usually it was a thriller. It gave me thrills just thinking about that word, as a kid. Thriller. Sometimes, my mom would turn back around to make sure I was sleeping, and I wasn't ever sure, if she could tell if my eyes were slightly open, or if she could somehow just sense that I had sneaky intentions.

While I was staring at the space between my parents' bodies, I realized that I would be thinking about that last scene with the golden boy for a long time. Forever. Upon reaching this realization, and looking at it, like an object in my hands, I wondered if it was as unwitting, as out-of-my-hands, as a realization, or if it was a decision. Conscious. A vow, a promise, a choice. Do not ever forget that moment. Don't you fucking dare ever forget that moment, when you looked up, from your cigarette, from your lap, from your friend's face, from your conversation, and multiple tiny things happened. You looked up. You saw someone walk up with a bike, lock up a bike, you knew it was him, in not even one full second of seeing him, the shape of him, backlit, his head, literally, backlit, like some fucking joke, the streetlight a halo behind his head, and you knew it, could feel it, there was no question that it was him, and he was facing you, but even more than that, you could sense that he was also seeing you, recognizing you, and you tilted or ducked your head slightly and squinted, to try to see better, you tried to change your line of vision so that he was not so perfectly backlit, so that you could see the evidence. You tilted your head, and you couldn't really see any better, but you knew it was him, and he knew it was you, so what did it matter?

I imagined a look of resignation, a half laugh, half sigh. Of course, this would happen, of course, this was how it would be. I imagined the feeling that he might take flight. He might do something like this, stop his bike, see me, and decide against it. That tenuous as things were, he had it in him, to steel himself against me, to say no, to back away. He had it in him, whereas I did not have it in me.

Finally, though, he had sat down next to me. I looked at his profile, the left side. This was what I was confronted with. But for a few seconds at a time, as we talked, he would turn to face me, and then I felt like I saw him, to see both of those light eyes, the long lazy lashes. His mouth, lips pursing, as he nodded at the noncommittal words we were releasing into the air. A woman walked by. We talked about the surface-most things, that had happened, that were happening, in our lives. Work. And yet, in all this, I couldn't shake the notion that in all this surface talk, we were both keenly aware of everything that lay beneath, that lay behind. As if for every superficial word of small talk, there was an equal and opposite reaction, or shadow, that was there below, or behind, adding weight, and we could both see that we both saw it, we wordlessly acknowledged it every second of the way, and it was somehow unbridgeable, this gap, between what we said and what we did in our regular public lives.

Later, on the walk back to the train station, the beginning part of it, I felt like a wild person. Half wild person, half numb robot. I was doing a sort of wary walking, looking all around me, as if now that this thing has happened, who the fuck knew what else might happen. Suddenly the world seemed very unstable. Suddenly, I did not know the world at all.

There was one last time, and one last guy, that I think about, that happened after that last scene with the golden boy, and before I left New York. At the top of the subway entrance stairs, before following this other guy down, I took a breath. Even then, I tricked myself into believing that the night still could end in a multitude of ways. I still believed that perhaps, I would decide not to have sex with him. I took in his apartment. I took in the hallways, the placemats. The posters on the wall, the lights strung up, these were all his roommate's. I sat on a stool while he made tacos. He was not from anywhere where anyone ate tacos, or made good tacos. I could tell that his tacos were going to be subpar, but I appreciated this unassuming guy making tacos for me, in the middle of the night. I looked at his movies. Wow, I said, you have a lot of romantic dramas. Yeeah, he said. He took me to his room. He led me by the hand. I did not like that he did this, or did not like the feeling of this. I wished it were someone else, leading me by the hand. He kissed me. He was very tall, had very wavy hair. His lips were dry and thin, and I put an end to the kiss. He took his glasses off, and looked very earnest. I shook my head at him, I made a noise of drunken frustration. I am so turned on by you, he whispered, while his cock was deep inside of me. Or, his cock was wearing a condom, and then wearing me. I hung on, by a thread. I hung on, by my very fingertips. I was left hanging, like an empty coat, on a coat-rack hook. On the coat-rack hook of his penis. I tried to make it funny, so that I could put off berating myself. He was exceedingly nice. I got my period on my trip to the bathroom, a surprise, one day early. He pulled my tampon out, put it on a napkin, lay a towel down on the bed. Soft hair, he said, mouth breathing lightly over my hair. Soft cheeks, he said, mouth on my cheek. Soft lips, he said, mouth on my mouth. I had never in my life done this thing, where I stayed over solely because I was too tired, where I stayed over even though the concept of it made me feel sick. But I did it then. I tried to remind myself to be calm, to step back, take a step back, be more casual, be less intense. Think, feel, react less intensely. This was what, maybe, I had wanted, or needed, to do, all my life. Be, and then be less. They advise this strategy when packing for travels: pack, and then take out half of what you've packed. That should prove sufficient. That shall lighten your load.

Strawberry fields whizzing by outside. My parents were talking now about the California condor. I was trying to fall asleep. This could be 1987 again, I am thinking, dreaming, sitting in the backseat of my parents' car, a lot of concerned talk about the condor. My dad tells me he heard that my reckless-driving ex-boyfriend from ten years ago has recently moved to London. Does that mean anything to me? No. Have it mean nothing. I tell myself these things: I am nothing. I am nothing, anyway, in the grand scheme of things, but here, now, I should just remind myself, that I am nothing, to the golden boy. Or, okay, not *nothing*, but not really anything exceptional. Or. Or, how about, I am, it was, as good as a seasonal fling. That is to say, as good as nothing. That is to say, nothing. That is to say, be a good, humble, Chinese person: round yourself down to nothing.

Once, in New York, I was crossing the street in a crowd of people, and brushed by an old man, who turned and yelled at me. Suzie Wong, he yelled. Go home, Suzie Wong. Somehow I knew he was calling me a prostitute. I'm not sure how I knew, but I went home and went on the computer to look it up, and confirmed what I knew: that Suzie Wong was a prostitute. It was a small thing that I felt—that she was a prostitute from a film—but still I knew it, felt it, in my bones. I looked it up: *The World of Suzie Wong* was the name of a 1957 novel by a British writer, and also a 1960 American romantic drama film, based on that novel, starring William Holden. The character Suzie Wong was a stereotypical hooker with a heart of gold; hypersexual, exotic, subservient. I'm not sure why or how I knew who she was. Even after reading about it online, I had no recollection of ever having read, learned, or heard about her before. But it was ingrained in me. Suzie Wong. That was who—what—I was, to that old man.

I wasn't sure where he wanted me to go. Maybe just away from him, maybe just away from that busy, chaotic, too-crowded crosswalk.

I began working in two restaurants, both in Newport Beach, one as a hostess, one as a pastry chef; both afforded me ample opportunity to stay out of my parents' house, and bond with coworkers who worked late hours, and liked to drink. A lot. The sous chef at one of the restaurants—who was perpetually sweating, and who had a pierced penis—and I went out drinking, a lot, and often. And then I would drive home. Wave to the security guard, wonder at the wet look of the asphalt.

Once, I was Skyping with my parents and the golden boy had just left our apartment, but he came back in because he'd forgotten his wallet or phone. Is that him?? my mom asked, peering out of the screen. Will you invite him to come to the Santa Barbara trip? My whole family, and my sister's in-laws, everyone was going for a week to Santa Barbara. No, I don't think so, I said. That's not him? Who is that? my mom asked suspiciously. Before I could tell her I'd been responding to her second question, she went on. Is that your gay friend Simon? You know, if you have so many guys hanging out all the time, he might feel like you're not serious. Don't you want to get married? Don't you have that dream?

I hate this. There is a sudden metallic taste in my mouth, from the way she says that word, dream, my saliva abruptly going sour and foul. I am having trouble swallowing, and somehow I can't hold it down anymore, No, I say forcefully. I do not have that dream. Why would I dream of that, I say angrily, looking at them, my mouth still, jaws stiff, throat tight. I clench my teeth not to stop from talking, but to hold onto something, to feel something solid, to close in on something hard. I don't fucking have that dream, or any other dream. I can't see it, I say. I can't see anything.

Sometimes, I thought about the golden boy's teeth, on the soft inner flesh of my upper thighs. I was flailing, in so many ways. I had never before bothered to notice how much I couldn't understand my parents, how much like aliens they were. Alien had never been a particularly interesting word to me before. But now, now I could see. Alienate, to make alien, could go both ways. To turn someone, or something, else into an alien. But also to make yourself the alien. That this could be an intentional action. Become something else.

In December, the week after Thanksgiving, we had a heat wave paired with a blast of late-in-the-season Santa Ana winds. The sous chef and I went to the Quail Hill multicinemashoppertainmentplex to watch *Saw III*, but we got there too late, so we got beers at the bar with a million beers while we waited for the next show. After, we went to The Quiet Woman, the bar on PCH that has the statue out front of a headless Victorian-looking woman, cradling her own head in the crook of her arm.

After The Quiet Woman. It's two a.m. I down a glass of water at the bar. You okay, the sous chef asks, patting me on the back. I nod. Take one deep breath. Two. We walk out the back exit to the parking lot. I shut my eyes for a few seconds to black out the whirling. See you at work tomorrow? he shouts, he is already across the way, at the next row of cars, walking toward his white pick-up truck, which seems to be glowing, a bona fide alien spacecraft. I know four other people who drive white pick-up trucks, because this is Southern California. Yeeaah! I exclaim, giving him a half wave. I stab my key at the lock in my car, several times, get in, sit down, adjust my mirrors, why, check my lights, check the gas. Halfway home, while I'm still on PCH, I find myself swallowing, swallowing. A sour kind of swallowing, frantic. My head is like an awful sandy cloud, filled with something putrid and green, but that is not what you're supposed to think about when you're driving back to your parents' house, drunk, and need to throw up, and the ghost of cold sweat is coating your body in a gross, creepy way. You're supposed to get it together. I roll down all the windows, turn the radio to 88.1, the jazz station. Handle it. You are already nothing, remind yourself that you are nothing. Because sometimes you forget. Sometimes you haven't been reminded, and you start thinking that you are something. I turn onto Chambord. I wave to the guard. I swallow, don't swallow. The gate clanks. The gate begins to part itself from the wall. It begins to roll, no sweat, all the time in the world. I blink. I wave my hand through the window, fanning in some outside air. I turn onto Bargemon. There is a parking space at the top of the hill, which I take, because even in my drunken state, I know better than to drive down the street all the way down the cul-de-sac to the actual house—my mother has ears like a jackal, the sound of the tires or engine or car door shutting in the suburban Provençal silence could wake her. I park. I can feel the vomit. I grab my purse, jump out of the car, start running down Cavaillon. Throw it up, throw it out, it can't be swallowed. Halfway down the street, I nearly stop, heave, doubled over. But I look down at the sidewalk, it's so white, and spotless. I look around at the empty street, the olive trees silvery, the French lavender poised and still.

The asphalt is black.

The lawns are perfect.

The sidewalk is so clean.

Everything is spotless.

There is not a sound.

I can't throw up here, I realize, this is not just some side street or alley. People will hear me. The neighbors. The live-in maids and nannies. There cannot be a splotch of vomit tainting the blank streets. This is Cavaillon. This is the chaparral of my childhood. This is a golden state.

I hold it. I resume sprinting.

The History Of Your Very Body

ONCE UPON A TIME, there was a hunter and a huntress who lived at the edge of a forest, just where the sand began, abutting a long, low desert valley. Long ago, in previous lives, the hunter and huntress had met, loved, lived in a city that stood at a moderate distance, its jagged rooftops and skyscraper antennae visible on the horizon for several weeks every fall when the air was cool and thin and clear. They had moved to a small home in the forest to make an escape. Sometimes an escape is a last resort, and sometimes it comes first.

&

The Story of the Huntress

Sometimes an escape is the story of two people, sometimes only one is left to tell the story.

There was a time, when she was still living in the city, when the huntress found that she had reached a point of peak beauty, peak prowess, peak child-bearing age, but she was trapped by the shape of her family. Years before, she had made a deal with her mother, that she would forever, unto her mother's death, be her interpreter, from Chinese into English, in all matters, in all interactions, in all intake and output of language. In return, she would be granted the flow of ancestral blood in her veins, the blood of a true huntress.

She would be an animal, fanged or feathered, claws and fur, eyes that tunneled through the dark at the speed of light, the most delicately sensitive nostrils, earlobes like James Bond microchip seashells. She would smell your blood even before you were born, and she herself would smell like blood. Her heart, it would grow to be small, contract wildly, to the size of a slim, sleek animal heart, the sturdy, knowing quiver of a rabbit heart, quick to scavenge, quick to ravage.

The huntress had been eager to agree to this exchange of languages, the giving and receiving of passports between worlds. Be gifted the gift to fuck all else. In the eyes of the huntress, the access to huntress blood was as close as she would ever get to being rid of her skin, the skin of a girl.

Bring me the snip of a puppy's tail, some snails, some entrails, rusted nails. The taste of animal is all blood, all texture. No girls allowed, no nice, no sugar, no spice.

Her salivary glands throbbed, filled.

❧

The Story of How to Carve With Vinegar

As a young girl, I couldn't be rid of my skin fast enough. I scratched and scratched, at the inside fold of elbow where tiny rashes formed, at the backs of my knees. Heat rash, eczema, dry skin patches, inflammations, ichthyosis, psoriasis, hives. Half of me was already a reptile, the other half that wasn't desperately wanted to be, craved new scales. Every chance I got, I took the class reptile home with me for the weekend. This was allowed with all the class pets; some years we had incubators and eggs and then little fuzzy chicks we could take turns borrowing for the weekend, or other years, butterflies or silkworms. A mulberry tree, giant, took up a large chunk of the enclosure that was the recess backyard at Bonita Canyon Elementary School. We tore leaves off, tossed them into shoeboxes. I dreamed of setting the cool, pale silkworms free, high up on the tree, what must it be like to live on top of and among your one provider.

I took home snakes. I took home iguanas. They were native to me, native to my surroundings, desert snakes, rattlesnake warning signs, sand, dust, lizards sunning on heat-scorched rocks. I held the iguana, felt its dry, fragile body, its small bones, beneath the wrinkled, thin papery skin. I dreamed of molting, shedding. My skin was so dry it cracked into tectonic plates, separated. Not just on my hands and feet, but on my arms and legs.

And then, many things at once. My period, a bleeding that wasn't, couldn't, didn't, seem like real bleeding. What was this? A monthly monstrosity, to be monthly cut down to size. Bleeding without a wound, unless I *was* the wound. Pimples on my face, angry, the perfect reflection of how I felt. Which came first, the anger erupting inside my head, or on the surface of my body? I wasn't sure. But I dreamed of being pure and perfect and smooth and new beneath it all. I began getting rashes on my feet, on my toes, between them. These small bumps turned into tiny blisters, that my mother diagnosed as athlete's foot. I was boiled down to two things, my body and my hatred. I wasn't particularly athletic, didn't even get to reap the social benefits of being an athlete, and now I had athlete's foot? My toes itched and stung, hot beneath my socks and shoes. The blisters sometimes oozed, dried, and cracked, crackled like caramelized sugar. Everyday after school, my ritual was to tear off my shoes and socks, my socks sometimes stuck to my feet at certain sticky points, a slight yellow brown stain where the rash scraped open had absorbed into the cotton sock, and go into the bathroom, hop up on top of the bathroom counter, and stick my feet into the sink, washing them one at a time with soap. Drying them off carefully. Applying more anti-fungal cream, or shaking on some sprinkles of anti-fungal powder.

At night, the ritual was more grim. After showering, I would go back downstairs in my pajamas, with a sweatshirt or blanket if it was cold, and it usually was, and from under a small side table, I retrieved a large glass mixing bowl filled with vinegar and covered in plastic wrap. I would tear off several paper towels from the roll on the countertop, and then I sat down in the darkened downstairs, at the dining table, in my usual chair, usually with homework or a book, and put my foot in the bowl. Usually it was just one foot or the other. Sometimes I switched out the vinegar with fresh vinegar from a large plastic jug of Heinz white vinegar. I watched the time on the oven clock, twenty minutes, but usually I sat for thirty or forty, desperate to be purified to the bone.

Sometimes I cried, a sour flood to the eyes, slowly dripping in streaks down my face. Mostly I read about blonde teenage twin girls with mirror-image dimples on their cheeks. Afterwards, I would look at my feet, temporarily not itching at least, not oozing, but pale softened wounds, tiny gaping craters where the blisters used to be, white-edged and soggy. I have faint scars on the tops of my feet still from those days, months, years. I don't know what eventually cured me, I think it was mostly a phase of my adolescent body, and I grew out of it, that it had to run its course no matter what ointment or home remedy my mother had me apply. But it was too late, because it was sitting there alone at that dining table, that began my inability to separate pain from healing.

Things that are curved sharp as white carvings:

- the whites of eyes, on either side, both eyes
- paper towels, quilted, perforated
- the edges of pages, books of fables, horror, how-to, nature guides, love stories
- the tip of the ivory dagger

When the huntress was a teenager, she realized that all girls carried the blood of beasts. Was it a negligible amount or just enough? Enough to know that being just half of some animal, being not quite something, seemed a curse. When she stood at the kitchen sink, helping her mother peel carrots, she dreamed of taking the wood-handled peeler to her own body, starting from the bottom of her feet, the long motion, the raw rocky sound of scrape, one take. Skinned in strips. Underneath, something pure, red jeweled pulp of blood, smooth white skin of reptile scales, a slither and a snap. All fall down. Clay soldiers tumbling over like strewn debris.

And so she and her mother made the deal. Seated at her old place at the dining table, the huntress rubbed her fingertips against the shape left from a small chipped-off piece of the veneer, that left a vaguely animal shape of a lighter wood beneath it. She imagined it a quadruped of some kind, vaguely shaped with smooth edges like an animal cracker.

There was no contract, no paperwork. Just the huntress, using her body as a bridge between her mother and anyone else, between one world and another world. Her mother had already ruined her in many ways, always telling her, you know, little doll, there is really no interiority in the Bible, and look how long those stories have lasted. The huntress took this to mean that feelings could be kept inside, and a story could still be erected in front of them, acting as an acceptable stand-in for intimacy, love, dimension, a life lived.

Her mother told her that Nathaniel Hawthorne was her real father, and other times that she was Rappaccini's daughter, and these two facts somehow did not conflict. Hawthorne and Rappaccini might as well have been the same old white man, white hair, wrinkled, thin papery skin, an austere seventeenth-century type, only ever existing in my mind in portraiture form, a cold marble bust, his hair a smooth hard helmet like the Ken dolls of the 1980s, his neck swathed in a combination of five different collars, cravats, neck scarves, and other pointy or starched or bunched up modes of swaddling, constricting, or bundling the neck. Only alive through his writing—his books or declarations or poetry or epigrams—which I read out loud or silently in my own voice, the ideas transferring from a page of paper into my body, passing into me, traveling through me like blood. The historical gap between me and them was so wide, so alien, that I was forced to use my own body, my own voice, as a stop-gap. Now you are mine, I thought.

The point being, that I didn't mind that this was the father that my mother tossed my way. It was kind of a dream come true, to have a claim to real America. Dreams of Puritans and hysteria and cold and barren one-room schools, in places like Massachusetts, places that were the entryway to America, which was pretty much the same thing as The American Dream. Places which were related to Plymouth Rock, and the Niña, Pinta, Santa Maria, and pilgrims and fire-and-brimstone preachers named James or Jonathan or George. Sinners in the Hands of an Angry God. John Donne. I wanted to be a plain girl, named Abigail, or Agnes, or Agatha, pure and plain, filled with piety, a dull wooden doll kind of girl, who somehow got filled with light, and filled with the flame of witchery or adultery, and delivered into a heavenly bouquet of flames. Cleansed by fire.

Instead, in my twenties, I castigated ex-boyfriends for the sins of their fathers, who sculpted tiny men with huge penises. And now, in my thirties, I myself was a sculptor, of women with huge pussies. I sculpted all the women I hated, all the current and ex-girlfriends of my current and ex-boyfriends, of my love, the hunter. It is an old story, to hate the other woman. It is so easy, after all, to hate the other, and to hate the woman. I never met the hunter's other woman, but I knew her. If we wander into the universe of fables, we know what we are to learn: what girls are made of (of nice, of sugar), and what boys are made of (of snipped off puppies' tails), and, well, the hunter's other woman, in this world, would have been made of the parts of a man, I would say: dark forest soil and the menacing wetness of green plants, incisor teeth dripping saliva, poised to puncture, and blood-matted fur.

After I conjured her ghost—I was curious, I couldn't help it, who was she, where did she get the balls—she would not leave. I had hopes I could stash her somewhere I didn't turn to so often, but she was always just at the periphery of my vision, always just in the whites of my eyes, which meant I was perpetually turning toward her, trying to catch a full glimpse. I have had other ghosts in my past; those ghosts all left. As I understood it, that's what ghostly things were supposed to do—be spectral, partial, fleeting, translucent in both space and time, only flimsily hanging onto a presence.

But the hunter's other woman ghost lingered. I'd seen photos of her before, on computer screens, on phones, paintings on gallery walls, in photographs in process, photo prints sunken on the bottom of developing trays in a community darkroom, wobbling under the weight, a face staring up from watery chemical depths, as if a pre-Raphaelite Ophelia. It did not prepare me for her presence in the form of the physical sensation of objects, of plant and animal parts. It was springtime, and everyday, as I walked home from work, staring up at the bare tree branches, the buds slowly butting out, slowly protruding their alien green tips, I felt her growing. When I got home, and cooked dinner, and sat down in front of nature documentaries, I could feel her staring back at me through the eyes of dam-busy beavers and lanky, light-on-their-feet wolves. At the end of the escape route, this is where one gets spit out. The filled green mountains of panda refuges in China gave me the feeling of leaves being chewed, prickling their ways inside my veins.

In all of her memories, the woman transforms into something fecund, something green and vital turning and twisting out of moist dark soil, or else a bird, a wolf, a predator, the fastest, most camouflaged thing, something with feathers or sharp teeth, a tough hide, shiny scales. The huntress changes and adjusts her memory at will, to ensure this outcome. Because, the next time she is given the once-over, elevator eyes dropping her to her knees, this is the tale she wants. And if her clothes are to be shed, you will see this narrative clearly written on every single visible inch of her body. And if she is to be chopped into two, split halves writhing, even then. Limbs thrashing, mind crazed and grasping at memories of past hours spent in a forest, in a city, with her love, the hunter, in a raging country—even then will her body tell you something that her tongue cannot.

The following stories have been previously published, several in slightly different versions:

"Monstrosity" was first published in *Timber* in 2016.

"Medusa Jellyfish" was first published in *Drunken Boat* in 2016.

"Stevie Versus the Negative Space" was first published in *The Offing* in 2017.

"The Closing Doors" was first published in *Flaunt* in 2012.

"I See My Eye in Your Eye" was first published in AAWW's *The Margins* in 2015.

"The Burgeoning" was first published in *Columbia Journal Online* in 2015.

"Year of Righteousness, Year of Confetti" was first published in *The Blueshift Journal* in 2016.

"The History of Your Very Body" was first published in *Queen Mob's Tea House* in 2017.

Acknowledgments

INVALUABLE THANKS TO: Allen Gee, Abbie Lahmers, Peter Selgin at 2040 Books; Mad Andrew Gifford and the team at SFWP; Mat Johnson; the literary journal and magazine editors and reading series organizers who have encouraged and supported me; Maxwell Williams; the Commitment; Columbia administrators, classmates, and teachers, especially those courses with Nicholas Christopher, Susan Bernofsky, Ben Marcus, and Elissa Schappell in which a number of these stories were formed/reformed; 92nd Street Y workshops with Christopher Sorrentino and Rivka Galchen; the Sackett Street Writers' Workshop with Jenny Zhang; the Asian American Writers' Workshop with Ed Lin; Vermont Studio Center, Art Farm Nebraska, and the Fine Arts Work Center in Provincetown for giving me time and space; Kundiman <3; and my parents Nelson and Grace, my sister Angie, and Neil, Sophie, & Ella, and all of my colleagues and roommates and friends and family who believe me when I tell them I'm a writer.

Photo Credit: Maris Hutchinson

BONNIE CHAU is from Southern California, where she formerly ran writing programs at the nonprofit 826LA. She received her MFA in fiction and translation from Columbia University. She has been awarded fellowships from Kundiman, the Fine Arts Work Center, the American Literary Translators Association, and Vermont Studio Center, and her writing has appeared in *Flaunt, Drunken Boat, The Offing, Joyland, Nat. Brut*, and other journals. She works at an independent bookstore in Brooklyn and is assistant web editor at Poets & Writers. Find her online at bonniechau.com.

Also from Santa Fe Writers Project

Bystanders *by Tara Laskowski*

"'Short story' and 'thriller' tend to be incompatible genres, but not in the hands of Tara Laskowski. BYSTANDERS is a bold, riveting mash-up of Hitchcockian suspense and campfire-tale chills."

— Jennifer Egan, author of
A Visit from the Goon Squad and *The Keep*

Magic for Unlucky Girls *by A.A. Balaskovits*

Fourteen fantastical stories take the familiar tropes of fairy tales and twist them into new and surprising shapes. These unlucky girls, struggling against a society that all too often oppresses them, are forced to navigate strange worlds as they try to survive. From carnivorous husbands to a bath of lemons to whirling basements that drive people mad, these stories are about the demons that lurk in the corners and the women who refuse to submit to them, instead fighting back—sometimes with their wit, sometimes with their beauty, and sometimes with shotguns in the dead of night.

My Chinese America *by Allen Gee*

Eloquently written essays about aspects of Asian American life comprise this collection that looks at how Asian-Americans view themselves in light of America's insensitivities, stereotypes, and expectations.

About Santa Fe Writers Project

SFWP is an independent press founded in 1998 that embraces a mission of artistic preservation, recognizing exciting new authors, and bringing out of print work back to the shelves.

Find us on Facebook, Twitter @sfwp, and at www.sfwp.com